The gigantic black hands on the town clock atop our municipal building inched toward twelve o'clock. Audie put a cell phone to his ear.

Cord and Penn, reprising their roles as Bob Grace and Dick Gaynor, burst through the saloon doors, shouting insults.

My heart stuttered a bit, worried for Cord. Penn sounded really angry.

"You can't get away with it. You're a scoundrel and a cheat." Penn's face was set into deep lines, hatred aging him prematurely.

"I'm not a cheat. I arrived first, fair and square. You have to accept it."

Tension twisted my shoulders. I held my breath.

"That's what you think!" Penn pulled out a Colt and fired.

A flash of light—popping sounds—*two* men fell to the ground.

Don't miss out on any of our great mysteries. Contact us at the following address for information on our newest releases and club information:

Heartsong Presents—MYSTERIES! Readers' Service
PO Box 721
Uhrichsville, OH 44683
Web site: www.heartsongmysteries.com

Or for faster action, call 1-740-922-7280.

Gunfight at Grace Gulch

Darlene Franklin

HEARTSONG
PRESENTS
MYSTERIES

"Thank you" is inadequate to my faithful critiquers: Susan Page Davis, Rhonda Gibson, Lisa Harris, and Lynette Sowell. I am proud to join your ranks.

ISBN 978-1-59789-677-1

Scripture taken from the HOLY BIBLE, NEW INTERNATIONAL VERSION®. NIV®. Copyright © 1973, 1978, 1984 by International Bible Society. Used by permission of Zondervan. All rights reserved.

Scripture taken from the King James Version of the Bible.

All of the characters and events in this book are fictitious. Any resemblance to actual persons, living or dead, or to actual events is purely coincidental.

Cover Design: Kirk DouPonce, DogEared Design
Cover Illustration: Jody Williams

Our mission is to publish and distribute inspirational products offering exceptional value and biblical encouragement to the masses.

Printed in the U.S.A.

1

April 1889

Dearest Mary,

How I have dreamed of describing for you the lovely piece of land that God has given us as our own. I truly believed the opening of the unassigned lands in Indian Territory was God's provision for us. At last I could leave my wandering cowboy ways and start my own ranch, with you by my side.

Last Monday I jostled with thousands of others stretched along the border to the unassigned lands. I wish I could send you a picture of the strange conveyances I saw gathered, everything from laden-down wagons to new-fangled bicycles. I stayed with trusty old Patches. He's seen me through many a scrape on a cattle drive, and I figured he could outsmart all those other horses.

Oh, Mary, how do I tell you? I failed! Patches flew straight and true through the dust-filled air. I cannot fault his speed. But others reached the land before me. I was unable to stake a claim on even the most miserable of the plots open for settlement.

Take heart, dear one. God must have another plan for us.

Your loving fiancé,
Robert Grace

Friday, September 20

The grandfather clock inside Cici's Vintage Clothing chimed two o' clock p.m. I strained my ears for the cries that would announce the arrival of Grace Gulch's two most famous participants in the 1891 Oklahoma Land Run. For once, I wished my store wasn't full of customers.

"Cici, look! They're coming!"

I hurried over to the customer who stood by the front window display of prairie bonnets. In minutes, the store emptied as effectively as if a fire alarm had sounded. I considered putting on my Edwardian hat but decided against it. People wanted to see the horsemen, not a bunch of feathers and ribbons. I joined my customers on the sidewalk to watch the race for Grace Gulch. I wouldn't cheer for either rider—no successful businesswoman could afford to show partisanship for either a Grace or a Gaynor in our town—but inside I rooted for Cord Grace.

Hoofbeats drummed the hard-packed earth. One horse, tall and black against the sky, crested the hill at the far end of the gulch. *Cord!* My heart raced at the sight of my childhood friend and persistent suitor. I might not want to marry him, but he looked every inch a hero on horseback. Seconds later, another horse, as white as the first one was black, appeared from a different direction.

So the cell phones worked. I bit back a smile. Unlike

the original race, the outcome would not depend on the fastest horse and pure luck. This reenactment was the brainchild of Audie Howe, interim director of the Magda Grace Mallory Theater—the MGM for short—named after the town's leading patron of the arts. In order to make sure that the right person won the race, Audie arranged to phone Penn Hardy, owner of the *Grace Gulch Herald*, when it was to time to move. Audie used every modern convenience to keep his plays running smoothly, even in telling a century-old story.

News of the reenactment had spread. Twice the normal crowd had come to town to celebrate Land Run Days. A sigh passed through the people gathered on the sidewalk. They cheered on their favorites.

"C'mon, Gaynor! Beat him to it this time!"

"You're the man, Grace! Get here first!"

"Yee-haw!" I couldn't contain my excitement any longer. My breaths came in short gasps as I wondered if, this time, history might be altered. Of course it wouldn't. Cord Grace could ride circles around Penn Hardy any day of the week. A working cowboy had all the advantages over a newspaper editor in a horse race. If they were riding for real, Cord and his horse Smoky would still come in first. Hands down.

The figures became bigger on the horizon. I could distinguish Cord's wide Stetson hat, his boots working spurs into Smokey's side. Behind him, Penn rode a bit like a proper English gentleman, upright in the saddle. He wouldn't get the maximum out of Starlight that way.

True to history, Cord and Smoky dashed down the path that would have been a tangle of undergrowth and leafy trees during the original run. Main Street stretched out from one end of the gulch to the other. Cord reined in his horse in the center of town and planted a flag in a small patch of grass.

"This claim belongs to Bob Grace!" Cord's voice rang with exhilaration. He sounded as pleased as his great-grandfather must have back in 1891. I released my breath, gasping in relief that the history of Grace Gulch would remain unchanged.

Penn Hardy, playing his ancestor Dick Gaynor, pulled Starlight to a halt beside Cord. "You're a dead man, Grace." He spat in the other man's direction. "You cheated. There's no way you left at the same time I did and got here ahead of me."

I allowed myself the luxury of booing with the audience. Of course I was booing Penn—er, Dick—for his unfounded accusation. But I might also be booing Grace for cheating on the land run.

Grace shrugged. "Smokey's a mighty fast horse. You might want to keep moving, if'n you want to stake a claim farther on." He nodded at the crest of the hill. Half a dozen riders appeared and galloped down the hill, ready to plant a flag on any unclaimed land. One of them represented my great-grandfather Billy Wilde, who founded the Crazy W Ranch after the run.

"You haven't heard the last from me," Gaynor threatened. He spurred Starlight into motion and headed down the main street in the direction of the far end of the gulch. Grace waited until he rode out of sight, then let out a rousing holler.

I joined with the crowd in clapping for the

performance. Cord grinned and bowed. "I worked up a mighty big thirst on that ride. I think I'll ask Miss Suzanne for a drink of sarsaparilla over in that fine eating establishment." He nodded in the direction of the Gulch. A false front had been added to the local café to convert it into the saloon it had been in early days for the duration of the festival.

People laughed, whether at Cord's overacted mannerisms or at the notion of a cowboy drinking sarsaparilla, I couldn't tell. I laughed along with them.

"So, Cici, you liked our little play," Audie Howe said. Sunlight glinted off his blond-capped head where he nodded in the direction of Cord's departing back.

Audie was dressed like a cowboy, and I had to admit that the man carried the part well. His neckerchief and hat showed the right amount of wear, and he appeared at ease in the outfit. Only his too-pale skin gave away his city roots. He wouldn't don stage makeup for this role, but he looked good, and I was glad the play turned out well for him.

"It seemed so real. I almost imagined it was the original Bob Grace and Dick Gaynor riding flat out for the gulch." I turned, enjoying the swish of beige silk flowing from the princess waistline of my dress, an original from the year Oklahoma became a state— 1907. "I wondered for a minute if we would have to rename the town Gaynor Gulch!"

"Why not?" Audie teased. "You have two of everything here. Why not two towns?"

Like most newcomers, he couldn't understand why a town as small as Grace Gulch needed two newspapers, two banks, and two community churches in addition to mainline denominations. That was easy, once you knew the history.

The land run initiated a lifelong feud between Bob Grace and Dick Gaynor. Anything Grace could do, Gaynor could do better. So he did. It broke his heart when the townspeople decided to name the town Grace Gulch.

"I confess that I wondered what Penn would come up with when he offered to write the play for the reenactment." The sun beat down on me as the crowd dispersed, and I wished I had worn my hat after all. "When he said he had access to correspondence between Bob and Mary Grace, I thought maybe he uncovered new information. If Bob Grace told anybody the full truth, it was his wife, Mary."

"In other words. . .did Bob Grace win the race fair and square?" After spending six months in Grace Gulch, Audie understood how important the question remained to our town over a hundred years later.

"Penn didn't show us anymore in the race today than we already knew. Grace arrived first." I smiled, reassured by that knowledge.

Audie's mouth twisted in a bit of a sneer. Maybe he wished that Old Bob Grace could be proven a cheat. Perhaps Audie thought that would give him an advantage over Cord, a Grace ancestor, in the romance department. Audie had asked me out a few times. More than a few times, to be honest. Last July we met during rehearsals for his first play in Grace Gulch—*A Midsummer Night's Dream*—when I helped with the costumes. After that, we fell into an easy friendship. We were part of the same Christian book club. Sometimes only the two of us showed for the monthly discussions, and people started linking our names.

That wasn't fair, any more than it was fair that people assumed I would settle down some day and marry Cord. For the first time in my life, I had two men competing for my attention. I was flattered. What girl—well, what woman knocking on thirty—wouldn't be? I knew thirty wasn't that old, but most of my high school friends were married with children by now. If I had to make a decision today, I didn't know which man I'd choose. In fact, I was going to a town barbecue with Cord tonight, and to the Land Run concert tomorrow with Audie.

"I see you have customers." The corners of Audie's mouth twitched. "See you tomorrow at the big showdown?"

"Wouldn't miss it for the world."

"*Au revoir*." Audie took my hand and kissed it, stepping out of his cowboy character for a minute. His eyes gleamed in appreciation.

I allowed myself a moment to celebrate the success of my feminine Edwardian dress, in spite of the nuisance of needing someone to help me fasten the eleven mother-of-pearl buttons up the back. My sister Dina came by long enough to complete the job this morning.

Now that the excitement outside had ended, I could see I had a full store again. A pint-sized customer stood in front of me, holding a red bonnet in her hands. She was adorable.

She must have sensed me watching her. "My name is Susie. I can't decide which hat I want." She picked up a green bonnet, as well. She smiled at me, and I imagined I was a schoolteacher gazing into the face of a pupil. Children were my favorite customers. If they could catch an interest in history through the clothing they bought in my store, they might tell the stories to following generations.

I looked at the bonnets. Both of them clashed with her orange T-shirt. "Which of them do you like better?"

I held back a smile to reflect her serious demeanor.

Susie twirled the hats, one in each hand. I could almost hear her thinking "eeny-meeny-miney-mo."

"The green one, I think." She grinned, emphasizing the freckles on her dimples. "Mom, can I have it?"

A woman hovered nearby, and the saleswoman in me kicked into high gear. "If you like the bonnet, why don't you show your mother the outfits over here? We have some ready-made dresses that are a perfect match for that bonnet."

I pointed out the rack of clothes, only to discover that the choices had dwindled throughout the morning. Time to restock. "Excuse me."

I went to the back room and grabbed for the supply of reproductions I had sewn in expectation of big sales for this year's Land Run Days. There was one, a lovely spring green, in the right size for my little friend. Her mother agreed to buy it along with the matching bonnet. The girl slipped into a stall and changed on the spot.

The hours whizzed by, and only when my stomach grumbled a complaint did I look at the clock and realize I hadn't taken a break. It was past closing time—eight o'clock in honor of the celebration. Most Fridays I closed at seven. People said the sidewalks rolled up in Grace Gulch at sundown. They didn't err by much. Only the Denny's on a spur from Route 66 and the movie theater stayed open in the evenings—and the theater operated only on weekends. Of course, the MGM also kept late hours when they were presenting a play.

After the last customers paid and left, I locked the doors behind them with a satisfied sigh. "What a profitable day." I smiled as I checked the visitors' log. I kept track of as many customers as possible to add them to my computer database. Most of the time Internet sales from my Web site provided my major source of income. A lot of today's visitors came from out of state, in addition to those from all around Oklahoma. When Graces and Gaynors learned we were recreating the famous feud, they made every effort to return to their hometown. Prospects looked good for future sales.

In preparation for the Land Run Days, I had forgone my usual practice of marketing authentic clothing only. There simply wasn't enough available. I had sold out most of my inventory by early September. Audie and my sister Dina, who volunteered as props manager at the MGM between college classes, had arranged for the loan of authentic period costumes for the reenactment. I was happy to oblige. Most of the town would do anything to help Magda Grace Mallory, the closest thing we had to royalty. Many of our town celebrities, including Magda, had purchased outfits as well. I had reserved one of my favorite finds for myself: the Edwardian beige silk I had been wearing all day, the lace-capped sleeves and square neckline a picture of grace from another time. It did nice things for my figure, too.

To accommodate the influx of business I expected, I had located patterns from 1891. I brought in fabrics that would have been used in that time period. People liked the idea of making their own clothing. I also spent hours churning out clothes in every style and size possible. Today made a sizeable dent in my stock, a good start to the weekend.

Thinking of the activity-filled days ahead, I hurried to drive home to my solid brick, two-story house in the center of Grace Gulch. Once inside, I put together a quick meal of leftovers then brought my food out to the wraparound porch. "Ah, my little piece of heaven." I enjoyed having my own place, away from my father's ranch, the Crazy W. By the time I ate a bite and hit the sack, I would barely manage my eight-hours-minimum before I had to arise again. At least I no longer had to wake up with the sun and fit my routine around ranch life, the way I had during the years after my mother died when I was thirteen.

Tomorrow, I decided, *I have to find a way to watch the gunfight.*

<hr>

As high noon approached, customers in my store started checking their programs and glancing at my grandfather clock. By a quarter to the hour, Cici's Vintage Clothing had emptied. Everyone wanted the best possible spot to watch the historic battle.

I exchanged the OPEN sign in my window for one that read OUT TO LUNCH—BACK IN AN HOUR. I locked the door and then threaded my way through the people, thankful for the police patrolling the crowds thronging the sidewalks. It seemed everyone was carrying a gun. Even the children held toy pistols. I could have stepped into another century. My dress's bustle—my Saturday costume—made maneuvering a bit difficult, but I found a spot at the front of the crowd. Across the street, my sister Dina leaned on the swinging door to the saloon. She waved at me and grinned. Today her hair was an impossible shade of red, which clashed with the magenta sweat jacket she wore. The last time I had seen her, the pink hue in her hair would have complemented the jacket. I shook my head. If I tried to dye my hair that often, it would turn into straw and float away.

I scanned the crowd for Audie and found him a few storefronts away from me. He looked anxious. He might never have a larger audience in Grace Gulch. An outdoor performance opened the gate for lots of things to go wrong. The actors never knew when people might step over the boundaries of the outdoor "stage." I hoped everything went well. He deserved it for all his hard work. Besides, I wanted him to succeed and put down roots in Grace Gulch. I caught his eye and gave him a thumbs-up. His stiff shoulders relaxed a fraction.

The gigantic black hands on the town clock atop

our municipal building inched toward twelve o'clock. Audie put a cell phone to his ear.

Cord and Penn, reprising their roles as Bob Grace and Dick Gaynor, burst through the saloon doors, shouting insults.

My heart stuttered a bit, worried for Cord. Penn sounded really angry.

"You can't get away with it. You're a scoundrel and a cheat." Penn's face was set into deep lines, hatred aging him prematurely.

"I'm not a cheat. I arrived first, fair and square. You have to accept it."

Tension twisted my shoulders. I held my breath.

"That's what you think!" Penn pulled out a Colt and fired.

A flash of light—popping sounds—*two* men fell to the ground.

2

September 1889
Dearest Mary,
   *I passed through Oklahoma Territory on the last
cattle drive. An opportunity has presented itself to me.
My good friend Ethan Hardy chose to seek an allotment
in Oklahoma Town. He is doing a good business with his
hostelry, and he has invited me to work with him.*
   *Tell me true, Mary. Can you see yourself the mistress
of a small home in the new city? A community ten-
thousand strong sprang up overnight. There is plenty of
opportunity for a man who is willing to work hard. I
know we dreamed of our own homestead on 160 sweet
acres, but this may be God's provision for us to begin our
lives as husband and wife.*
   Awaiting your reply.
   Your loving fiancé,
   Robert Grace

Saturday, September 21

The seconds dragged on. . .too long. Neither man
got up from the ground. Dead silence fell on the crowd,

as though they were collectively holding their breath. No one had died in the original gunfight. Falling to the ground carried the reenactment too far. *What was happening?*

I found myself racing across the street. As much as a woman *can* run wearing a bustle. A figure dashed past me. Seconds later, I arrived at the place where the two men had fallen, a tableau from a movie where a hazy crowd shouts silent cheers and the camera zooms in on the star.

Audie had reached them ahead of me and crouched beside the fallen men. No one else had moved.

Cord stood up, dusted off his black Stetson, and looked down at Penn.

Cord's not hurt! Fake blood stained his shirtsleeve where the original Bob Grace had been shot in the arm. For a second, I felt nothing but overwhelming relief. Then reality clicked in. If Cord was okay, then what about—

"Come on, Penn—er, Gaynor, you can get up now." Cord grinned. Playing the part of Old Bob Grace had given him the thrill of a lifetime.

"I think he's. . .dead." Audie glanced up, his face ashen.

"What? Naw, you know it's just fake blood." Cord touched his own wet shirt where the blood bag had burst, creating the appearance of a nasty shoulder wound. Neither one of us wanted to believe Audie's pronouncement.

Cord bent down next to Penn's body. I held my breath.

"He's—he's really dead." Cord affirmed Audie's assessment.

I tried to kneel next to Cord, but the bustle at my back got in the way. I settled for leaning over. A small hole had been drilled in the center of Penn's worn leather vest. I pressed my hand to my thudding heart. I'd seen that type of wound before, but not like this. They always marred the beautiful skins of the deer my dad hunted each fall.

I bent forward to see better and collided with Audie as he stood. My hat—today a red teardrop-style—flew off my head and landed at Audie's feet.

"Where are the police? We have to tell them that there's been a terrible accident." Audie picked up my hat and dusted it off before returning it to me.

"Police? Accident?" Cord stared at the gun in his hand as if he didn't know where it had come from. "No, Audie, you have it wrong. Whoever's bullet did this didn't come from my gun. I was using blanks. You know that."

"*We'll* figure that out, if you don't mind." Ted Reiner, chief of Grace Gulch's four-person police department, joined us in mid-street, with female officer Frances Waller.

For the first time since arriving by Penn's side, my mind registered the crowd. They remained frozen in place, looks of puzzlement on some faces, horror on others. Mothers with small children scurried down the sidewalks, hiding the all-too-real violence from their young eyes. Dina huddled by the swinging saloon doors, her eyes wide with fright. At least she hadn't run out into the street to join us. I saw a few other familiar faces at the saloon. Suzanne Jay's bouffant blond hair looked even stiffer than before, as if fear had frozen it in place. Ronald Grace, the mayor and Cord's cousin, talked to Mitch Gaynor, the editor of the *Sequoian*. The tall newspaperman gestured widely to the bald, short mayor. I wondered what spin they would put on today's events. Pastor Waldberg preached—really, that was the only word to describe his posture—to a small cluster of people I knew from church. He was probably lecturing them on the need to prepare to meet their Maker.

I took a deep breath and looked once again at Penn's body. Frances, surgical gloves covering her delicate pianist hands, watched Dr. Barber as he examined the wound on Penn's chest. She and I knew each other from way back. "I'll set up the perimeter," she told the chief.

Ted Reiner represented the worst of the police profession. Loud, obnoxious, a good old boy, he welcomed opportunities to throw his weight around. Like now. "Wonder how this happened. You put on a show, and look what happened."

"I believe it was an accident," Audie responded to Reiner's comment. Did I hear a trace of intolerance in his voice? Perhaps his director's eye cast Chief Reiner in some Keystone Kops routine.

Reiner turned his attention to me. "Why did you run into the street? Did you see anything suspicious?"

"No, I was just afraid. . ." No, I couldn't say that I was afraid Cord had been hurt. Two men had fallen, after all. Even though I didn't voice the words, I felt heat coloring my cheeks. "I was afraid someone had been hurt. The two weren't supposed to fall to the ground, you see, and—"

"Humph." Reiner turned the sound into an accusation. "I'll need that gun, Cord."

"It wasn't my gun that killed him. Look for yourself." He held the gun in the palm of his hand but didn't let go. "Why aren't you canvassing the crowd, looking for the real shooter?"

"We'll do that. I still need your gun. And we need you to come down to the station."

"Why? I didn't do anything!" Cord sounded desperate. Frances took the gun in her gloved hands.

"We'll need your fingerprints for comparison, Cord." Frances interjected a note of reason to Reiner's request. "What about you, Cici? Audie? Did either one of you touch anything?"

I shook my head.

"I checked for a pulse, that's all," Audie said. "I saw the blood. It was in the wrong place. He was supposed to receive a fake leg wound in the gunfight."

Reiner frowned. "You'd better come with us, too." He turned accusatory gray eyes on me. "We'll take your statement later today."

"Sure. But don't you want to speak to the crowd? Someone must've seen some—"

"I was just about to do that." Reiner placed his hands on his hips. He'd probably dreamed all his life of getting to boss around a crowd of people like a real city cop. Not much in our small town had prepared him for the actual experience.

"If I can have everyone's attention!" he shouted. His announcement rippled through the crowd in waves, creating silence in its wake. "There has been an accident. Please stay where you are until one of our officers has spoken with you. The remainder of today's play has been cancelled. The town barbecue will be held tonight as planned."

Noise whispered across the street. A few people shook their heads and drifted away, but most waited their turn to speak with the police.

Cord remained in place, arms stiff as if a pair of handcuffs might materialize on his wrists. "Will I still see you tonight?" he asked me. "If they let me go, that is."

"I wouldn't miss it," I said. "This is just a formality."

Eventually Dr. Barber had Penn's body moved to his clinic—which doubled as the medical examiner's office—and the crowd disbursed. By the time I closed my shop at six that night—another banner day for sales, driven by people curious about the gunfight "incident"—I had tired of saying, "I'm not at liberty to talk about it right now." At least later I could talk over the events of the day with Cord, my escort to the town barbecue.

Cord was picking me up at seven thirty. I needed a full hour to change from the dress and bustle of the day to another period costume, a woman's gym suit. What better time to wear the athletic attire than an informal barbecue? The outfit, black bloomers popular in the 1890s beneath a black and red wool skirt, promised to be warm, and I could secure my hair in a braid. A lovely double cape completed the ensemble if it turned cold, although I didn't expect it in September.

Cord would be as eager as I was to discuss the day's events. Sometimes—well, let's be honest, most of the time—he accepted the Grace mystique. As a Grace of Grace Gulch, he considered himself above suspicion, even if only on a subconscious level. Chief Reiner's grandmother on his mother's side was a Gaynor. Today's tragedy placed a Grace—Cord—in the power of a Gaynor—Chief Reiner. The feud was alive and well, over a century later.

I was neither a Grace nor a Gaynor. My own great-grandfather arrived minutes after the famous pair during the land run. Wildes had ranched in Grace Gulch since the beginning and stayed neutral in the feud, profiting from both sides.

Our neutral stance in business matters didn't play a part in the friendship that sprang up between the Graces and the Wildes, and eventually, Cord and me. Our ranches shared a common border, although the Grace spread was much larger than ours. We'd done everything together, from riding sheep at the rodeo as children to attending our senior prom. Then Cord went to OSU while I traded in two years at the community college my sister now attended for two years at a fashion design school in Houston. People assumed Cord and I would tie the knot someday.

I wasn't so sure. I couldn't marry Cord when Audie Howe also made my heart race. Cord was like my brother, a warm quilt when I wanted the comfort of the familiar. But Audie. . .

No, I refused to think about Audie tonight. Cord

had invited me to the barbecue first. I had accepted his invitation, and I intended to enjoy myself.

Dressing in period costume gave me an excuse to avoid wearing makeup. Taming my wild dandelion hair into a single braid took all my time until Cord rang the doorbell.

Cord dressed like he always did—in blue jeans and a plaid shirt, newly pressed in honor of the occasion, a jacket lined with sheepskin, and his favorite black Stetson on his head. "Your steed is ready, ma'am." He had teased me about renting a "surrey with the fringe on top" in honor of the barbecue. I confess I felt a tad relieved to see his usual blue pickup in the driveway.

He didn't bother to help me into the truck. Good thing I had exchanged bloomers for the afternoon's dress and bustle.

"How long did they keep you downtown?" I asked.

He smiled his melt-your-heart smile that made girls swoon. I wondered if it covered up insecurities tonight, as it often did.

"Not long. They took my prints, like Frances said. Reiner thinks I shot Penn on purpose. Of all the muleheaded. . ." Thunderclouds darkened his eyes, erasing the smile.

"Now, Cord, Reiner can't help being Dick Gaynor's great-grandson." I hoped to bring that smile back to Cord's face.

"Maybe not, but he doesn't have to be a mindless fool," Cord muttered.

We arrived at the park a couple of minutes later. Fresh paint shone on playground equipment, and the grass remained green thanks to a summer of watering. Plenty of people had gathered already. Small tents formed a square. The saloon, aka the Gulch, grilled hot dogs and hamburgers; two other restaurants offered brisket and ribs. Free drinks were served in the fourth tent. Families displayed their favorite barbecue side dishes on a center table. Beans, potato salad, fresh watermelon, and chocolate cake. I added my contribution, coleslaw with a bit of onion in it. Nothing like a community get-together to catch up with old friends. Unfortunately, today's event had an extra edge, as townsfolk passed on gossip about Penn's death.

"We're here," Cord announced to no one in particular. As the current Grace of the Circle G Ranch, he sometimes expected events to be put on hold until he arrived. No one returned his greeting.

With the unexpected developments over the noontime gunfight, I hadn't eaten lunch. My stomach reminded me when we neared the barbecue pit and the scent of savory spices filled my nostrils.

"Come on. I want a hot dog." I pulled Cord in the direction of the Gulch's tent.

"I'll go to the other tent for ribs later," Cord said. He waited good-naturedly while I queued up to the tent.

Suzanne Jay, the well-preserved blond from the saloon reenactment, took my order. The consummate professional, she smiled at everybody. "Anything for you, Cord? Too bad what happened today." Clearly doing her best to dispel his dark mood, she put a couple of blackened hot dogs into buns and pointed to the condiments lining the shelf. "You have a great night."

Shoulders slumped, Cord didn't respond.

We walked across the grass to the opposite tent, my mind reeling with what I might say to convince Cord that Penn's death was an accident—surely, no one held Cord accountable. But before I could form a thought, we passed two clusters of familiar faces, and nobody greeted us.

Cord ordered his ribs and hurried through the line at the center table. I dawdled, debating which dishes to sample. By the time I finished, Cord had spread a blanket out on the grass. He fetched tall glasses of iced tea and sat. The thunderclouds had returned to his eyes.

I finished the first bite of hot dog and swallowed. "Cord, you've got to stop blaming yourself for—"

"Don't you see how everyone is avoiding me?"

I knew Cord liked to be the center of attention, but he didn't usually carry things this far.

"No one wants to talk to the *murderer*," Cord said.

Surely people didn't think that about Cord! They couldn't. "It is rather awkward, I suppose. Even if the bullet came from your gun—"

"It didn't."

"—it was still just a horrible accident."

Cord glowered at me.

"Hey y'all!"

I would know that voice anywhere, anytime. It

had scolded me every day of life until I was thirteen. My older sister, Jenna, popping in from out of state for one of her unexpected visits. She lived in Taos, New Mexico, where she made a living as a computer programmer and art dealer. Jenna squatted next to us on the quilt as if we had seen each other yesterday instead of eighteen months ago. She was everything I was not, her hair a perfect blond, aided by a bottle, I thought spitefully, and windblown into perfect curls around her face.

"What *is* that outfit you're wearing, Cici?"

"I'll have you know that it was the height of fashion for the athletically inclined lady."

"A hundred years ago."

"More like eleventy ten, 1894." We giggled at the phrase we had picked up from Tolkein and hugged. Jenna had that effect on me. One minute she infuriated me, the next we chatted like friends at an all-night slumber party.

"I didn't know you planned to be here," Cord said. Cord had known my sister all his life. "The last I heard, you were in New Mexico someplace."

"Taos," Jenna said. "But I couldn't miss out on *all* the excitement. I flew in today. The stupid car rental agency didn't have my car ready; I asked for a Subaru, and they tried to give me a Ford. Can you imagine! By the time I got them straightened out, it was too late to get here for the showdown at noon, so I went ahead and ate lunch at this divine little Mexican restaurant I discovered the last time I was in Oklahoma City. Then I kind of lost my way wandering down Route 66. I just got to Grace Gulch an hour ago, and the first thing I hear is that Dina is in trouble. What happened?"

It took a minute for Jenna's words to register. She did tend to rattle off facts machine gun-style, and it took awhile for the important ones to sink in. "Dina, in trouble? What do you mean?"

"Well, the police suspect her of substituting real bullets for blanks in the gun. As if she would do something like that."

"Where did you hear that?" How could my sister be in town for less than an hour and already know more about the investigation than I did? Trust Jenna to ride to Dina's rescue when I was here for her all the time.

"Jessie Gaynor." Jenna gestured with a bakery box from Gaynor Goodies. "She told me when I bought these cupcakes."

That explained it. The bakery storeowner ran the town's gossip mill.

"Do you mind if I join you?" Mitch Gaynor, Dina's boss for the summer at the *Sequoian* after Hardy had turned her down at the *Herald,* towered over us. He sat without waiting for further invitation. "Jenna, welcome home."

Uh-oh. Business, not friendship—because frankly we *weren't* friends—brought Mitch to our corner of the picnic. Of course, the newspaperman wanted to talk to us.

"I want to get your account of the accident this afternoon." Mitch confirmed my suspicion. "For tomorrow's paper. You were first on the scene, I understand?"

You know perfectly well we were. You were there, too, standing right in front of the Gulch watching us.

"The chief told us not to comment," I said.

Not discouraged, Mitch turned to Cord.

Hand raised, Cord shook his head

"Can you at least tell me if you checked the bullets in your gun before you went out to put on the play?"

"Don't you go accusing Dina," Jenna spoke hotly.

"Of course I did. I'm no actor who relies on the props girl to get it right." Cord shut his mouth, probably wishing he hadn't spoken quite so openly. At least not where the family of the props girl could hear.

Mitch grinned, and the saliva in my throat turned to molten lava. Fingers had started pointing at the two people with the best opportunity to kill Penn—my dear sister Dina and my old childhood friend.

3

June 1890

My dearest Mary,

God is good. I heeded your wise advice and did not accept Hardy's offer of work. Rumors abound that the Cherokee Commission will negotiate a settlement with the remaining tribes located in Indian Territory. Once they agree on terms, additional land will be made available for settlement. Of course the natives may protest the sale, but they have little choice. Since Congress passed the Dawes Severalty Act three years ago, pressure on President Harrison increases almost hourly to open all Indian lands.

I intend to make the run every time it is offered until we have our own land. As God is my witness, I promise that it will not take long.

Your loving fiancé,
Robert Grace

Saturday, September 21

The last bite of hot dog turned to ash in my mouth and my appetite fled.

Mitch continued to pester us, but after Cord's outburst, none of us said much. "If you want to know about the props, why don't you ask Dina yourself?" I asked. Mitch's interruption of our dinner peeved me. "After all, she works for you."

"Oh, I will, don't worry." He whipped out a camera and snapped a picture of us before we could protest. "That's a fetching outfit, Cici, I must say." He grinned again and slid away in search of another victim.

"He as much as called me the murderer," Cord sputtered.

"You *and* Dina." I looked at my plate. The sight of the perfect watermelon slice that tempted indulgence fifteen minutes ago now soured my stomach.

"Where is Dina tonight?" Jenna asked. "I can't believe she'd miss the barbecue."

"At work. She called to say Mitch asked her to help get out a special edition of the *Sequoian*." I shook my head. "So she's hard at work and missing all the fun, and he's here bothering people for interviews."

"I bet she's glad she didn't get that internship at the *Herald* that she applied for. Things must be in an uproar at the paper after Penn's death." Jenna kept up on the town gossip in spite of the fact she had kicked Grace Gulch's dust off as soon as she finished high school and never looked back. As they say, you can leave Grace Gulch, but Grace Gulch never leaves you.

No one else came our way during the barbecue. Jenna finished eating and left us alone, giving us a few moments' privacy, but we didn't stay for long. Cord drove me straight home and let the engine idle.

"Will I see you tomorrow?"

I cringed. Although we attended different churches on Sunday mornings, our families sometimes spent the afternoon together. Maybe he expected me to attend the Land Run concert with him tomorrow.

"Perhaps. I'm going to the concert with Audie." I tried to keep my tone nonchalant. I almost wished I hadn't made those plans. Cord needed my support now more than ever.

Now it was Cord's turn to frown. "Another time, then."

"Do you want to come in for a cup of coffee?" The day had disturbed us both in a myriad of ways, and I wondered if he wanted company. But he agreed and helped me climb down from the cab of the truck.

While my favorite decaf caramel truffle coffee brewed, I set out a pair of gray ceramic mugs with a painting of our state bird, the beautiful scissor-tailed flycatcher doing a sky dance on the sides. I was eager to speak with Dina, but the clock told me she would be hard at work. I'd have to postpone the call.

I thought Cord might want to talk, but he didn't say much while we drank the coffee. Neither one of us wanted to voice the thoughts prominent in our minds. Penn's death. The two people with the best opportunity to kill him were my sister—who handled props for the play—and Cord, the man sitting across my kitchen table, who had fired the gun. After he finished his coffee, I offered him a second cup, but he shook his head.

"I'll be heading home." He stood up, hat in his hands, and stared at the floor for a long minute. Then he looked at me with a forced smile. "At least you aren't afraid to ask me into your home."

"Oh, Cord, of course not."

He motioned with his hand. "It's okay. I'm sure even Reiner will figure out that I'm innocent. Eventually." He said his good-byes and left.

I checked the clock and decided I could call Dina. I picked up my handset and punched the speed dial for Dina's cell phone.

"Hey, Cic, what's up?"

Rolling presses clattered in the background.

"Can you get away from the printer?"

Dina laughed. "Sure. Several people showed up for work after they left the barbecue. I can take a short break." The clattering subsided, followed by the slam of a door. "Is this better?"

"Are you alone?" I didn't want anyone at the paper to hear even part of our conversation.

"Yup. I ducked into an empty room. Why?"

"How did things go today with the police? Did you ask for a lawyer?"

"Why? I haven't done anything wrong. They asked a few questions, took my fingerprints, and let me go."

"What did they ask about?"

"You know, like when did I last handle the guns."

"Well? When did you?"

"I was there when Penn and Cord picked them up. About eleven thirty." She paused. "I can't believe Penn's dead."

"Me either."

"Do they think Cord's gun killed him?"

I didn't answer her question. "When was the last time

you checked the guns? You know, put the blanks in?"

"We used blanks at the rehearsal last weekend. We test fired all three guns and decided on which ones Cord and Penn would use during the performance. Everything went off without a hitch. I checked them one last time that morning. Everything looked good." Her voice rose in pitch. "Hey, why all the questions? I did my job!"

"I'm sure you did. But somebody shot Penn. With a real bullet. Did you have a chance to check the guns after the fight?"

"No. The police took both guns—Cord's and Penn's. But I'm sure there were blanks in both. If someone had changed blanks for the real thing, wouldn't Cord have been shot, too?" She sighed. "Maybe not. They used the same guns each time. All somebody needed to know was which one was Cord's and which one was Penn's."

I knew what Reiner would say. Cord could have switched the bullets and killed Penn on purpose. He didn't have a motive of any kind, but that wouldn't stop the chief. Cord could speak up for himself. But if they dug around for Dina's motive, on the other hand. . .

"If the police want to speak with you again, be sure you have a lawyer there."

"Cic." The rise in Dina's voice told me I had pressed far enough. She'd complained to me often enough that I was trying to take her mother's place. Truth be told, I did feel like her mother since my mom died back when I was thirteen.

I only hoped she would heed my advice. What

were kids coming to these days? Didn't she watch any of those endless cop shows? I sighed. Little sisters didn't like big sisters butting in—any more than I appreciated Jenna—but I couldn't worry about Dina's feelings right now.

I heard some talking in the background. "Hey, I'd better get back to work. We have to finish up here, or else I'll never make it to church in the morning."

By the time we said our good-byes it was close to midnight; Sunday had almost arrived. Maybe this week Pastor Waldberg would preach a comforting message instead of his usual hellfire and brimstone. Everyone in Grace Gulch still suffered from shock at Penn's death.

My alarm woke me out of a deep sleep shortly after dawn the next morning. I needed to be up extra early to get ready for another hectic day, starting with getting dressed. Although I wore period clothing throughout the week at my store, I rarely did so on Sundays. After all, Christians set aside the day to worship the Lord, not to do business. Most weeks I alternated combinations of my limited contemporary wardrobe of four skirts, seven blouses, and three sweaters.

But today many people would dress up in honor of the festivities. They had purchased their clothing at my store and wanted to wear it as often as possible during Land Run Days. It would look odd if I didn't wear something appropriate for the occasion. So I took the time to dress carefully. I selected a gray bolero jacket over a white blouse, a lace jabot with a matching skirt, and a derby hat.

By the time I finished dressing, my doorbell rang. My father stood outside, a trim figure at sixty, handsome in his workaday blue jeans. "Would you like a buggy ride?" His eyebrows wiggled. "Or did you forget?"

Dina, wild red hair a shock over her high-necked blouse, leaned forward in the carriage and waved. I stared at the buggy. On the back of the carriage, a sign read "CELEBRATE LAND RUN SUNDAY WITH US AT THE WORD OF TRUTH FELLOWSHIP." After yesterday's tumult, I had forgotten that my family had volunteered to drive the buggy around the neighborhood inviting people to worship with us. But Dad appeared at my doorstep this morning as if nothing out of the ordinary had happened.

"We have doughnuts and hot chocolate," Dad added as an extra inducement.

My stomach rumbled its agreement. "Sounds great. I haven't eaten breakfast yet." I smiled in acquiescence— the church was counting on us—and grabbed the double cape I had worn last night. Dad handed me up to the worn leather seat and then urged our horses forward.

We circled the church three times during the Sunday school hour, waving at everyone we saw and inviting people to church. Some asked if they could ride the buggy, and Dad explained that rides would be available for all ages—after the morning worship service, while they were preparing for the picnic on the grounds.

A few minutes before service, Dad unhitched the horses from the buggy and hobbled them near a tree on the church lawn. As full as the parking lot was, I wondered how many people had crowded into our sanctuary and if we could find a seat. But Audie greeted us at the front door with a smile and said, "This way." He managed to save a spot for us.

Audie sat with us most weeks, ever since his first Lord's Day in Grace Gulch. I looked forward to seeing him on Sunday mornings. I flashed a "thank-you" smile in his direction as Frances—the cop was also our church's pianist—began the prelude.

Well-worn booklets titled *Gospel Hymns* replaced our usual hymnals in the pews. Leafing through, I saw some of my favorite hymns, a nostalgic treat from my childhood before contemporary worship music became the norm. The praise team looked strange in their long dresses and fancy suits, tambourines replacing electric guitars. They led us through several gospel songs. What songs we didn't know, we stumbled through in merry spirits. Audie seemed to know most of the music.

"I see that Ira Sankey wrote a lot of these songs. He traveled with the evangelist D. L. Moody, you know," Audie whispered to me during the offering. "In Chicago I grew up singing this stuff, since it was his home base back in the day."

The song service ended all too soon. Enid Waldberg, the pastor's wife, led the children's Sunday school class in reciting the Twenty-third Psalm from the poetic King James Version. Then Pastor Waldberg stood up to speak.

The bulletin announced the sermon title as "Life Is Short—Are You Ready?" For the past few months, Pastor Waldberg had emphasized the importance of evangelism on this Sunday, when we expected an influx of visitors due to the Land Run Days. I was sure he had prepared his sermon well in advance of yesterday's tragic events, but Penn's death only emphasized his point. Our pastor's thick black brows protruded over somber dark eyes, his mighty voice and piercing gaze adding weight to his usual hellfire-style. In spite of his occasional odd traits, he truly was the best preacher I had ever heard. He invited us to open our Bibles to the sixteenth chapter of Luke, to the story of the rich man and Lazarus.

Waldberg read the passage and opened in prayer, then began to speak.

"Some people would say Penn Hardy was well off, like the rich man in Jesus' parable. He was rich in the things of this world. He owned a newspaper. He belonged to a prominent family." The Gaynors in the congregation preened themselves at the reference. "And he ran his newspaper fairly, reporting as much of the good news as the evil doings of this generation. He will be missed as a deacon of our church.

"But this day—this day! His soul has been called to account. You never know when your life will end. If Penn could, he would send an angel to warn you of wrath to come! But God says no! If you don't believe the Word of Truth, how would you believe an angel sent by God?"

And on he went. God's Spirit was with him. Several

people raised their hands during the invitation. I felt guilty that I longed for comfort instead of conviction on this particular day, when God was in the business of saving souls.

After the service, I sought out Enid Waldberg. A warm, cozy woman, she served as the perfect counter-point to her husband. I complimented her on the great job the children had done. Audie, as usual, dived into a discussion about the finer points of the sermon with the pastor.

"As Oscar Wilde said, 'Ordinary riches can be stolen, real riches cannot. In your soul are infinitely precious things that cannot be taken from you.'" Audie never missed an opportunity to quote his favorite playwright. "Lazarus knew what real riches were. I hope I can emulate his example."

Pastor Waldberg looked flustered. I didn't blame him. Audie's use of a quote from a reprobate to echo a spiritual truth would make any man of the cloth uncomfortable.

"Or as Proverbs says, 'Wealth is worthless in the day of wrath, but righteousness delivers from death.'" Audie added the scripture verse to put the pastor at ease. His knowledge of the Bible exceeded his knowledge of great plays. I admired a man who knew his Bible backwards and forwards.

"Yes, indeed." Poor Pastor Waldberg looked a bit shrunken. If they held a memory verse contest, Audie would probably win. He seemed to have the entire book of Proverbs memorized, chapter and verse.

We stayed for the picnic, held in celebration of Land Run Days. After so much food sampling over the weekend, I might have to let out my clothes before I wore them again.

"Are you sure you don't want to run the buggy around?" Dad invited Audie to drive.

"Not unless you want a runaway horse."

"No, we can't have that. I'll take the buggy around a few more times before I eat." Dad donned his hat and climbed up in the seat.

Audie took off his jacket and added red suspenders over a white shirt. "Let me duck inside and get ready for my act."

Audie might not be comfortable holding the reins of a horse, but he could act. He had offered to be a mime at today's lunch, and I knew he planned to add white face makeup and become a blond Marcel Marceau for the afternoon. He reappeared a few minutes later, a gaggle of balloons tied around his waist, and the children on the grass swarmed around him. He mimed each animal as he tied the balloon. I loved his passion for bringing his art and joy to everyone.

Audie reminded me of those two brief years I went to college out of state, of art and history and a whole other world, a world that I explored through dresses of the different eras. He was as skilled at theater as Cord was at ranching, but he bucked the actor stereotypes by being down-to-earth, concerned, and authentic.

The two men differed in so many ways. Cord was as familiar as a foam mattress that conforms to a person's shape over time. My experiences matched his. Everything I could do around a ranch, he could do as well—make that better—as I could. Cord already knew all my most embarrassing moments. There were no secrets between us. But that was the problem. Did I want more of the same?

Both men had hinted at taking things to the next level, to making it an exclusive relationship. I thought it strange that Cord never cared about that until Audie entered the picture.

My eyes strayed to Audie while I picked at a piece of fried chicken. He had stopped tying balloons and started miming Bible stories. He tied a napkin around his head and lifted his eyes to heaven. Then he sprinkled coins in the children's hands, sending ripples of giggles through the crowd. He pointed to the billboard of the ten commandments Pastor Waldberg had added to our lawn and then pointed to himself. He pondered each commandment. Yes, I do that. No, I don't do that. He made his self-inventory clear through head motions and facial expressions.

I didn't recognize the associated story until Audie took off the napkin and threw dust in his hair. He looked down at the ground. Of course! Jesus' parable about the Pharisee and the tax collector.

"Stop daydreaming and come and eat." Dina touched my elbow. "Dad's taking a break from the buggy rides."

I grabbed a glass of lemonade and joined them at the end of a picnic table, daydreaming about two different men. Times like this I missed my mother. Who else could I talk to about matters of the heart? Dad assumed I chatted with Jenna about "girly things," as he put it, but she lived far away, and we didn't phone that often.

Besides, with the mistakes she had made, I couldn't trust her advice when we were younger, and now we didn't talk much. Then there was Dina, but at nineteen, she was inexperienced. So I prayed and asked God to show me which man was right for me. If either.

Audie must have seen us sit down, because he mimed eating and left behind the protesting children to go through the buffet line.

Of course, people asked me about what happened yesterday. Several others stopped Audie on his way to our table. They must have asked him about Penn's death as well, because I saw his answering actions and movement.

Dina caught me watching Audie. "You're staring." She poked me in the arm. The point of my plastic fork dug into the side of my mouth, and I yelped.

"Guilty." I dabbed my mouth and took a sip of lemonade. "I wonder what he has to say about what happened yesterday. Because we haven't had a chance to talk about it." I chased a last bite of potato salad around my plate.

"Oh, is that all?" She noticed my empty plate. "I'm ready for a second trip. What do you want? I'll get it for you."

"I'd like a small spoonful of that tamale pie."

"Sure, be right back."

Audie broke away from another questioner and moved in our direction.

"You can have my seat." Dina stood up and offered her chair to Audie.

Somehow, Audie had juggled two cups of tea with

his plate. He downed one in a few long gulps.

"I didn't know miming could work up such a thirst."

"Answering everyone's questions did that." Audie grabbed a second glass. "I feel like I should record my answer. Push '1' for 'Is it true that Cord shot Penn?' Hit '2' for 'Do you think someone substituted real bullets for the blanks?' And so on."

"Grace Gulch hasn't had anything as traumatic as this in years. People are horrified that one of our leading citizens was gunned down in broad daylight." We grimaced at each other.

"How did things go for Dina with the police?"

How thoughtful of Audie to ask. I looked at my sister, winding her way between the laden tables. "Okay, I guess. I wish she had brought a lawyer, but—"

"Hey, Dina!" One of Dina's friends from high school—home from college for the weekend—called out as my sister approached our table with plates in hand. "You really should be more careful with those props." The words fell into a moment of silence.

Dina paused mid-step, her face as red as her hair. Then she continued walking to our table, head held high.

I was never prouder of Dina than at that moment. But someone had to figure out the truth about Penn's death, before the town dragged Cord and Dina's names through the mud more than they had already.

July 15, 1891
My dearest Mary,
Praise God! I felt your heart rejoice with mine when I heard the news that negotiations with five of the tribes in Indian Territory have begun. They must make their own arrangements and take a census to determine land allotments. Hopefully each tribe's lands will open individually as soon as they sign a treaty with the government. The lands are lush, Mary. I wish I could pick a posy of thistle and lace to bring to you. The day the land is mine, I will bring you flowers every day, if you like.

I have headed to Indian Territory so I may be on the spot as soon as President Harrison sets the date for the next land run.

Your loving fiancé,
Robert Grace

Sunday, September 22

After the church picnic, I arrived home only minutes before Audie stopped by to pick me up. I forgot my questions about the investigation in the warmth of the MGM lobby, where most of the town gathered for the afternoon concert presented by the Land Run Celebration Choir. For now, I would concentrate on enjoying the next couple of hours in Audie's company.

A curlicued playbill displayed in front of the theater had advertised the concert for weeks. Someone on the Land Run Days Planning Committee discovered a program from the original theater, the one that was destroyed by a tornado before the MGM was rebuilt on the same site, and decided to duplicate the music of that era. The director dug through piles of old music and promised a gala, roaring '90s style.

Suzanne, theater diva and temporary saloon hostess, greeted us at the door. "I'm so glad you could join us today." She handed each of us a program, a work of art with gold tassels dangling between blue velum covers. Inside, sepia ink was printed on cream parchment.

"Your seats have been reserved at the front." Suzanne's attempted smile looked like a reflection in a cracked mirror, unexpected from Miss Sunshine of the MGM theater group.

"What's wrong?" Audie asked.

So I wasn't the only one picking up distress signals.

Suzanne's smile faltered. "It's just that. . .well, you know, with Penn's death. . . It's so awful."

"It is terrible." Audie nodded, appearing to take her words at face value, but I wondered. Penn didn't act with the theater on a regular basis, and I didn't think Suzanne knew him all that well.

"But the show must go on, right?" Suzanne smiled, this time a genuine dazzler that showcased her acting talent.

"So you're going ahead with the surprise?" Audie's mouth quivered with mischief.

"Absolutely!" Suzanne arched an eyebrow and lifted the hem of her dress, revealing a hint of beribboned bloomers. "Go on in. Enjoy the show."

"What surprise? Is there something I don't know?" I scanned the program: solos, choir numbers, a barbershop quartet, and even a dance number—all familiar. I had helped the choir director with the costumes and thought I knew all the acts.

"Let's just say we added a little something extra at the end."

"We? I thought you stayed away from this production." Content to orchestrate the reenactment, Audie had left the concert to the choir director—or so he'd said.

Audie shook his head. "Suzanne suggested it, and I put the idea to the director. He agreed. Let's go ahead and find our seats."

We made our way to the front, where Audie had a reserved place as interim theater director. Dad and a freshly dressed Dina had found seats toward the back. She waved a cheery hello and didn't seem any the worse for the encounter at lunch. The seats had sold out weeks before; any latecomers had to be satisfied with SRO. A rousing success for the first musical performance at the new theater.

Magda Grace Mallory never did anything halfway.

She'd rebuilt the edifice with all the bells and whistles. Red velvet hung from the walls. Soft light from sconces suggested candlelight instead of electricity. Cherubs draped in scarves adorned the ceiling. Audie once admitted to me that the acoustics were horrible. People didn't care, carried away by the Paris Opera House-style beauty.

I sank into a plush seat at the front. Next to me, Mitch Gaynor claimed a front row seat as a theater critic, and so did Mayor Grace on the other side of Audie. I felt sorry for the people sitting behind them. Mitch's height would block their view of the stage, and the spotlight would bounce off the mayor's bald pate. One front row spot remained empty, probably the place Penn Hardy would have occupied. I shuddered and thrust the thought away.

"Good afternoon." Dressed in a white linen suit, Mayor Grace beamed at us with the bonhomie that made him such a good politician. "I am truly looking forward to this afternoon's performance. You did an amazing job with the reenactment, Audie."

"Thank you, Mayor."

"Until the unfortunate accident. A terrible tragedy."

"A great tragedy, indeed," Audie said as he shook the mayor's hand. "Penn was a good man."

"And a great newspaperman. I'm not ashamed to admit it," Mitch added. "Grace Gulch has lost an icon with his passing."

I buried a laugh with a cough. Everyone knew Mitch hated Penn's editorial guts.

Conversation stalled as Mrs. Mallory appeared in front of the curtains to welcome the audience. The lady had class; she wore a gown that could have graced Prince Edward's consort. She greeted all comers, prettily thanked the music teacher from the high school for leading the program, and departed through the wings. The curtain opened on a nineteenth-century paradise, a summer day. A few trees added a touch of reality to the painted backdrop, with a small pavilion to the side, for solos and quartets and such, I supposed.

The concert began with "Oklahoma!" Of course, what else? The singers sounded every bit as good as the Mormon Tabernacle Choir.

"Now that I live here, I know what Hammerstein meant when he talked about the wind whipping down the plain," Audie whispered to me as he stood to his feet, clapping along with the rest of the audience. "After that brush with a tornado last month."

"You can't tell me the wind never blows in the Windy City," I whispered back.

The first half of the program consisted of sentimental favorites from 1891. Audie encircled my shoulders with his arm, and I leaned against him, enjoying the music.

Enid Waldberg led a female barbershop quartet. Her throaty contralto voice lent itself well to the melody in "The Pardon Came Too Late." The melancholy message of the song sent a shiver down my spine, and Audie's hold on me tightened protectively. I hoped that the lyrics didn't presage some awful ending to yesterday's events. *Don't get carried away.* No one had been accused, let alone convicted.

With the final selection, "Every Rose Must Have

Its Thorn," the curtain closed on the first act. Audie and I found our way to where Jenna had joined Dad and Dina at the back.

Jenna saw Audie and flashed a neon smile. *Oh, no. Why didn't I see this coming and prepare for it?* Any male under fifty drew my older sister's attention. And Audie was a better-than-average specimen.

"Well, will you look at that," Jenna said. "Cici, where have you been hiding this hunk of man flesh?"

This was even worse than I had dreaded. I felt heat soak my cheeks.

"Audwin Howe, interim director of the theater. And you are. . . ?" Audie recovered well. Maybe the theater inured him to flamboyant sirens. He arched an eyebrow in my direction, waiting for an introduction.

"This is my sister. Jenna. Wilde." I tried, really I did, to make that one single sentence. I couldn't help it if each word came out on its own.

"I flew into town for the festivities," she purred. "You're not from around here, are you? I'd remember you."

"I'm from Chicago originally, although I'm hoping to settle down in Grace Gulch."

That statement made my heart flutter. Audie looked in my direction and spoke my name, breaking Jenna's spell. "Would you like something from the bar?"

I could have kissed him then and there. It took a strong man to resist my sister's charms. "I'd like a glass of water with lemon, please." I headed for the ladies' room while Audie made his way through the crowd to get the drink.

Audie was leaning against a Corinthian column

when I exited the facilities. He must have sensed my earlier discomfort about Jenna's overtures. "Don't worry. I'm deaf to the siren song. 'Musical people always want one to be perfectly dumb at the very moment when one is longing to be perfectly deaf.' "

"Don't tell me." I had to laugh. "Oscar Wilde again?"

"Of course. I had a drama teacher in college who pounded Wilde into our heads. He had a lot of wit, if somewhat lacking in the wisdom department. And speaking of laughter. . ." He gestured toward the doors, where we could see the lights blinking to signal the end of intermission. "The second half is supposed to be comedy. There were a lot of comic operas in that time period. Some real classics that you don't hear very often nowadays."

"I can't imagine why"—I consulted my program— " 'Boom Ta Ra' isn't a standard on the oldies station." We rejoined the mayor and Mitch in our front row seats.

A circus tent replaced the summer garden scene. As it turned out, "Boom Ta Ra" was hilarious. Clowns chased each other around the stage on outrageous unicycles, honking horns with every repetition of the chorus. Next came cats and dogs—children dressed in costumes, their names listed in the program—for "Johnny Doolan's Cat."

The next to last song was a coup for our concert. Magda Grace Mallory had pulled strings and obtained permission to perform "Oklahoma Rising," written especially for the recent Oklahoma Centennial by native sons Vince Gill and Jimmy Webb. The lyrics that touched on everything from the Dust Bowl to the bombing of the Alfred P. Murrah Federal Building brought tears to my eyes. When the band played the introduction to the national anthem, patriotic fever surged through the auditorium.

The director turned to the audience and invited us to join in singing "The Star-Spangled Banner." A huge flag was lowered behind the risers. Several hundred voices rose in song. I could have jumped up on the stage all by myself and hollered, "God bless America," and sung "Yankee Doodle Dandy." I didn't want the concert to end.

Others must have agreed with me. Someone in the back shouted, "Encore!" and the audience took up the chant. I caught Audie in a private smile, and I had a sneaking suspicion that the call for an encore had been a plant. I recollected his strange conversation with Suzanne.

A young girl ran across the stage and whispered in the director's ear. The auditorium hushed.

The director spoke to the audience. "I've just received word that vaudeville sensation Belle Ormand has arrived, straight from Paris, France! And she is prepared to share a song with us." He clapped, and soon we were applauding, as well. I heard a few cat whistles from the energized crowd.

Suzanne strutted on stage, her dress scandalously short for the 1890s. From where I sat, I could see the ribboned bloomers that adorned her calf muscles. In a nasally voice worthy of Miss Adelaide in *Guys and Dolls*, she sang into the mike, "I'm the belle of high society. . ."

"Ta-ra-ra. . ." Clanging cymbals and the bass drum announced the chorus as the choir joined in singing. With each beat, Suzanne kicked her legs high in the air.

I gasped. "She's doing the—"

"The cancan!" Audie grinned. "Her idea."

The entire auditorium sang along as Suzanne kicked her way across the stage. Rhythmic clapping took over, and I sensed movement behind me. I turned my head. Someone was dancing down the aisle. Jenna! With a laughing Dina at her side, both of them pumped their legs in time with Suzanne. If a trap door opened beneath my feet, I would have fallen through with thanks.

The director noticed the commotion and paused the music. He bowed and invited my sisters on stage. Dina grabbed my arm and dragged me with them. The director turned to the audience. "And now another special treat—the Wilde sisters!" Suzanne smiled and retreated to the wings. Lifting his baton, he led the choir in another chorus. "Ta-Ra-Ra Boom-De-Ay!" crashed across the stage. The three of us linked arms and kicked.

I can't tell you how I survived the next few minutes. With my skirt and bustle, I couldn't lift my legs as high as I used to in marching band. Dina and Jenna, experienced dancers and dressed in slacks, moved easily. I stumbled around after them, lifting the edge of my skirt with the toes of my shoes. "Just you wait," I muttered to Dina beneath the loud music. She lifted her head high, laughed, and kicked some more.

After endless repetitions of the chorus—Audie told

me later they only sang it twice more—the music stopped. In the front row, Mitch Gaynor jumped up and started applauding. The auditorium joined him in a standing ovation. The director clapped along with them.

"Thank you all for joining us today. And a special thank-you to the Wilde sisters for making it a most memorable event."

The Wilde sisters. That was us, all right, in more ways than one.

Audie reached us first, congratulating me with a hug and a brush of his lips across my burning cheeks. "Well done!"

I tried to make my way out, but everyone surged forward, eager to speak to Suzanne or the director or one of the Wilde sisters. I gladly let my sisters take the spotlight.

Dina's eyes sparkled, the unpleasantness from lunch long forgotten, and I couldn't begrudge her high spirits. I realized I hadn't once thought about Penn's death or the police's suspicions since she dragged me on stage. Maybe some good came from her latest stunt after all.

"If you want to escape. . ." Audie said, sotto voce.

I nodded, and he said, "This way." He led me toward the actors' entrance at the back. The air felt cool after the hot auditorium, and I shivered. He draped my cape over my shoulders and slipped his arm through mine. We walked the perimeter of the theater. Ahead of us, around the corner, we heard voices. The lighter trill of a female voice placated the deep rumble of male voices raised in anger. It took me a minute to identify them. My heart sank. Ted Reiner and Frances

Waller were quizzing Cord.

"Mad cow? My herds are perfectly healthy!" Cord sounded like a petulant schoolboy trying to prove he hadn't cheated.

"We've seen reports that indicate otherwise."

We stopped moving forward, unwilling eavesdroppers to the conversation.

"If you have any further *questions*," Cord said in a dismissive voice, "you can talk to my lawyer." The sound of boots stomping the ground grew fainter.

I started forward. Audie stopped me.

"It's none of our business."

I struggled against Audie's arm. "They're looking in all the wrong places. I've got to talk to them."

He glanced in the direction of Cord's retreating form and sighed.

"Wait a minute. . . You don't think *Cord* did it, do you?"

"I don't know what I think." He dropped his hand from my arm. "Go on. Talk with Reiner. Anyone who can dance the cancan in a bustle and heels can take on the chief."

We rounded the corner in time to see Frances speaking into her walkie-talkie. Reiner was not in sight.

"Cici. Audie." Frances seemed surprised to see us.

"We missed you at the concert," Audie said.

"I had to work." Frances shrugged. "Crowd control for Land Run Days had already stretched the department thin, and now with the inquiry into a suspicious death—"

"So, then. . ." She had given me the opening I was looking for. "You haven't ruled out murder?"

"It's looking more and more like murder," Frances admitted.

I plunged ahead. "We couldn't help overhearing your conversation with Cord. Something about mad cow?"

The chief joined Waller on the lawn. "That's official police business." No more easy answers—Reiner would not welcome my interference. "I'm glad you're here, Cici. I need to ask you some questions."

"Yes?" Maybe I could guess the direction of the inquiry from his questions.

"I understand that your sister Dina had a disagreement with Mr. Hardy shortly before his death. Something to do with an internship?"

"She was turned down for the position. What does that have to do with anything?" My stomach clenched. Two weeks ago, Dina, the tips of her hair dyed flaming orange for fall, had interviewed with Penn Hardy. She told me all about it later, upset when he denied her the much sought after short-term job at the *Grace Gulch Herald*.

"Did she or didn't she threaten Mr. Hardy when he refused to hire her? I believe she said: 'You'll be dead before I ever read your newspaper again.' " Reiner read the menacing words without emotion. "Is that correct?"

My stomach clenched again, squeezing in pain. "I

can't tell you. I wasn't there."

But I knew what Dina had told me. And Reiner had the quote word perfect.

July 30, 1891

My dearest Mary,

I fear that I was overly optimistic in my earlier estimate of the available land. I have spent much of the last days exploring the territory. It is true that it is as green as an African jungle. Water abounds. That is the problem. Spring rains bring flooding. The rivers flow in an awkward fashion, first wandering north, then east, and then south, often crisscrossing the same plot of land. Farmers will be at the mercy of the most recent thunderstorm. Doubtless the Indians will keep the already-cleared lands for themselves.

I pray daily that God will show me where He wants me to establish our future home.

Your loving fiancé,
Robert Grace

Sunday, September 22

A few minutes later, Audie tucked me into the passenger side of his Focus. I liked the sedan, a welcome change from Cord's pickup. Low clouds rolled in from the west and dripped water on the windshield like a leaky faucet. I couldn't stop shivering, and I knew the wet weather wasn't the only reason. Audie turned on the heater.

"They suspect Dina. And Cord." I stated the obvious.

"They have to question everybody. It's nothing personal."

"But they're concentrating on Dina and Cord. It's like they're digging for a motive why either one of them wanted Penn dead."

"Did Dina really threaten Penn?" Audie didn't sound suspicious, only curious. How could he be so blasé about something so important? Of course, Dina wasn't his sister.

"She may have said something in the heat of the moment. But you know Dina. Overly dramatic, just like her. . ." I stopped myself in time. I needed to tell Audie about my sister, but not right now. "She didn't mean anything by it."

"I can imagine." Audie's lips twitched in a smile. "Reiner hasn't learned Oscar Wilde's secret of life."

"What is that?" I wondered what Wilde had to say about a police officer.

"Why, 'the secret of life is to appreciate the pleasure of being terribly, terribly deceived.' Reiner is blinded by the obvious—Cord shot at Penn, and Dina loaded the gun. He's not looking any further."

I gazed out at the flat, gray landscape. The rain washed away whatever joy remained from the concert after the confrontation with the police. I had looked forward to Land Run Days for months, only to have tragedy and suspicion fall on people close to me. What could I do to make things better?

"Are you willing to help Cord? It would mean a lot to me."

Audie shot a look at me and then returned his focus to the windshield. "What do you have in mind?"

"We could ask Cord about the mad cow rumor. Do you mind if we stop by the Circle G? It's on the way to Dad's place." I regretted the suggestion as soon as I made it. What kind of woman asked her date to go visit another man?

"I guess so." Audie sounded resigned. He drove past my street and headed out of town in the direction of the ranch. "I've heard the term mad cow, but I confess I don't know all the details."

If Audie didn't mind the side trip, then I shouldn't worry about getting him together with Cord. I gave him a straightforward explanation.

"The scientific name for mad cow is bovine spongiform ence-something. It's a disease that attacks a cow's brain. Recently a version of it has transferred to humans. That's what has everyone scared. So far it's only been found in Great Britain and a few other places."

We reached the turnoff for Cord's ranch. "Are you sure you want to do this? It could be dangerous."

"Cord, dangerous? Audie, I've known the man all my life."

"Looking into a murder is dangerous." His blue eyes turned to ice.

I could see Audie was less than thrilled by the idea, but I just had to talk to Cord face-to-face. "If someone doesn't look for the truth, an innocent person will be accused. Like my sister."

Audie grimaced but turned his Focus onto the gravel road. It was designed for pickups, not passenger cars. Wet gravel spit up under his tires and pinged the front windshield. I wondered what Cord would say about the rumors. He did some business with a British cooperative last year, but I was sure he'd had all the animals screened.

A few feet up the road, we encountered the familiar sight of a solid *G* filling a circle atop a sturdy steel gate. We had reached the entrance to the Circle G Ranch.

"Pretty fancy," Audie said.

"They earned it. The Circle G has been known for quality beef since early days."

"How much farther is the ranch house?" Audie asked after a quarter of a mile.

"A few more turns in the road. The Graces bought up land when other families moved out during the Dust Bowl. It's a big spread." We passed a few horses near a feeding trough. They kept their noses down and seemed oblivious to the rain.

"I don't know a thing about ranching. Or horses. Or cows." Audie looked at the mares. "I feel like a kid driving out in the country who points to every passing animal. 'Look, Mom, horsey.' "

"That's okay," I said. "There's more to life than farm animals and crops. Like beauty and art."

"Perhaps." Now we were passing cows huddled together in a pasture. "But this is so much more. . .I don't know, elemental."

A figure on horseback approached the cows. Cord atop Smoky. He spotted the car and made hand motions, indicating that he would meet us at the ranch house. We rounded a final bend and came upon the sprawling building.

Audie scanned the area that was so familiar to me. As well-known as my own home. Pioneer Bob Grace had built a sturdy house with an open veranda out of native stone; and generations had added to it since.

Cord must have taken a shortcut, because he arrived right after we did. I saw him on the other side of the corral. Smoky's haunches bunched, and he jumped the fence in front of us. Cord slid off the horse in one fluid motion. He motioned for Audie to roll down the window.

"Go ahead in. It's not locked," he said. When he tipped his hat, rain poured from the spout of his waterproof brim. "I'll take care of Smoky."

Show-off. Audie's shoulders slumped, as if considering his own lack of ranch skills. Cord and I competed in junior rodeos as kids, and we both won our share of gleaming belt buckles. I had packed mine away with my childhood toys. Cord's still lined the mantelpiece above his fireplace, along with his medals for marksmanship.

Audie removed his jacket and handed it to me. "I can't offer to carry you over the mud." He grinned. "But you can hold my jacket over your head to protect that pretty hair and fancy hat."

Did Audie really think my dandelion hair was pretty, frizzed as it must be in this weather? We made a dash for it, rain plastering Audie's pristine white shirt to his well-muscled chest. The few yards to Cord's front porch felt like miles. I kicked off my shoes and left them on the porch, unwilling to track mud into his living room.

We opened the door, and I flicked on the light by the door lintel. Since his mother's death, Cord had remodeled the interior of his home into a hunting lodge. Mounted heads of half a dozen different animals roared from the walls. A large bear rug warmed the floor, and I knew—from Cord's endless bragging on the subject—that the furniture was made with genuine bison leather. "Best thing for the buffalo," he insisted. "If we domesticate them and raise them for commercial use, they'll never suffer extinction." He had a point, but I found the atmosphere forbidding. So did Audie, who looked as out of place as the Connecticut Yankee at King Arthur's court.

"Did he kill all those animals?" Audie asked. He studied the placard beneath the head of an eight-point stag. "First kill."

I nodded. "He bragged about that deer for weeks. He was only thirteen at the time."

I hurried into the kitchen, where the gentle spirit of Cord's mother still made itself felt in warm yellow curtains and stoneware mugs. I lit a fire under the kettle and headed for the pantry in search of teabags and coffee.

Audie followed me in. "You seem familiar with the place."

"I should." I frowned. "I've been in and out of here since I was a kid." I found the coffee, Cord's favorite, a dark French roast, and started the coffeemaker.

"Not much choice of tea," I said. "Orange pekoe. Some herbal teas that look like they're years old. There is some hot cocoa mix if you want it."

"I'll wait for the coffee." Audie picked out a plain blue mug and held it between his hands.

"I see you made yourself at home." Cord came in through the back door and hung his wet things on a peg like he had when we were children.

I opened the cookie jar, a pottery cow that Cord had given his mother one Christmas, and found what I expected. Chocolate chip cookies that Cord made from frozen dough he bought at the store.

Cord poured himself a cup of coffee. "Sit down. To what do I owe the honor of your company today?" His eyes darted in Audie's direction.

What should I say?

Audie surprised me by taking the lead."We over-heard part of your conversation with Reiner today."

"Oh, which part was that? When he practically accused me of shooting Penn on purpose? Or when he said my cattle had mad cow disease?" Cord grimaced. "Stupid man. I can't believe he asked me in public like that. Just the hint of mad cow could ruin me. Rumors like that spread like a grass fire."

"But they're healthy?" What if the rumors were true? My family's ranch shared a boundary with the Circle G. How did it spread? *Silly girl.* I stopped myself from chasing tumbleweed thoughts.

"Of course they are." Cord looked hurt at the slight suggestion of my suspicion. He bit off half a cookie, chewed it, and then swallowed. "Look, this is what happened. You know that I traded breeding bulls with a cooperative in Britain a couple of years back. Penn found out that some cattle in the district where the cooperative is located came down with mad cow. He said that my herds might have contracted the disease." Cord shook his head.

"Did he blackmail you? What did he want?"

"Nothing as blatant as money. Penn said that if I bought more advertising in the *Herald*, maybe he could dig a little deeper and disprove his facts. Otherwise he would run the report he had."

I was horrified. Did Penn really sell the news to the highest bidder? "What did you do?"

"I told that dirty newshound what he could do with his rumors." Cord grunted. "Let me show you something." He disappeared through the living room door in the direction of his office.

"Well. It sounds like Penn was not quite the 'icon' that Mitch called him this afternoon."

Audie poured himself a cup of coffee. "We might as well follow him." He walked back into the living room.

Trailing behind, I didn't know what to say. I thought back over a lifetime of news events. Penn couldn't slant national or international news, not with twenty-four hour a day news networks. But what about local news? I shook my head. Grace Gulch's grapevine worked too well for any reporter to tell an outright lie.

Cord stomped into the room and slapped some pages on the table. "Take a look. This is what I showed that nosey reporter."

I looked at the letterhead from the Oklahoma Department of Agriculture.

"I'm not irresponsible," Cord complained, as if someone had accused him of that very thing. "My busness; associates in Britain warned me as soon as the problem cropped up over there. I had my vet check my herds and sent a report to the state Board of Agriculture."

I scanned the document. It was dated a year ago and gave the Circle G herds a clean bill of health.

"No one is going to spread lies about me and get away with it." Cord slapped the desk with such force, I jumped. For a second he looked like the kind of man who could commit murder.

Audie looked as shocked as I felt.

"Sorry, bad choice of words." Cord took a swallow of coffee and groaned. "I told Penn that he could print his lies if he wanted to, but I'd slap him with a libel suit before the ink dried on the printing press. He backed down when he saw the report."

"Why didn't you tell Reiner about this when he asked you?" Audie frowned at the report, eyebrows bent in concentration.

"I didn't want to talk about mad cow where everybody could hear us, did I?" Cord downed the rest of his coffee. "I'll take the report to the police station tomorrow."

"No wonder you put such feeling into the reenactment." Audie grinned. "The feud has been reborn."

"It did feel good to beat Penn in that race." Cord relaxed a bit. "But I didn't kill him. Reiner's going about this all wrong. I couldn't have shot Penn, not the way it went down, even if I wanted to."

A small voice inside me spoke up. *He had a gun.* I didn't believe he shot Penn, did I? I had to admit that he had the opportunity. Unless someone else substituted real bullets for the blanks, and that brought suspicion back to Dina. There had to be another answer.

"I've been thinking about it." Cord shook his head, a few damp curls sprinkling water in the air. "To be honest, I haven't done much else since yesterday. I went riding to clear my head." He shivered.

"Let's start a fire before we talk anymore," I suggested. "All of us are wet."

"Good idea. I'll take care of it." Cord lit the kindling already stacked in the fireplace. Soon cheery flames danced in front of us. Audie lifted his hands before the fire as if trying to catch their warmth. His shirt had almost dried, but it still stuck to his back in patches. Cord settled back in his recliner and put his feet on the footstool.

Seeing the two men side by side, I was struck by how different they looked in spite of their similar blond good looks. Cord's hair curled, whereas Audie's fell in artfully styled straight lines. Cord's blue eyes shaded toward navy, while Audie's were the color of a limitless clear sky. Cord's sun-burnished skin was darker than Audie's strong Viking features. Powerful muscles rippled across both their backs. In a town full of handsome cowboys, perhaps I had taken Cord's friendship too much for granted. I could hear Jenna's voice. *You got that right.* I snorted in my coffee.

"Are you all right?" Audie asked.

"I'm fine." My voice sounded even while my heart raced. How had I missed the similarities between them before? Maybe because although the two men looked alike, their occupations and personalities lay at opposite ends of the spectrum. Why either one of these handsome men should be interested in plain old me, I couldn't guess.

"Have you come to any conclusions?" I wanted to get my mind back on the investigation. Thinking about the two men confused me. "What about the shots? You know about marksmanship." I glanced at the medals on the shelf.

Cord sat up, the recliner footstool retracting into the chair with a thud. "Yes, I think so. Let me show you what I figured out."

He directed Audie and me to stand a few feet apart in front of the fireplace. "I was facing Penn like this. We drew our guns and shot at each other, like we rehearsed. But then I heard a bullet whiz by my right arm, from behind me. I thought it was sound effects. . . until Penn didn't get up." He backed up until he was slightly to the right of the front door. "The shot came from this direction."

"The saloon," Audie said.

"The Gulch," I said, simultaneously.

I felt a hundred pounds lighter. Tie a stone to my foot, I was ready to float off the floor. Someone else fired the fatal shot.

But that meant—murder. This was no accident. My spirits crashed, and I shivered in my still damp clothes.

"Have you told the police about this?" Hopeful, I searched Cord's face.

"C'mon." Cord shook his head. "Reiner wouldn't listen to me. He'd tell me that they have their own experts and that I'm trying to save my own neck."

Audie muttered something under his breath. I caught the word "feud."

"I have hopes that Frances will figure something out." Cord brightened. "She's got a good head on her shoulders."

"If the police won't do anything about it, I will," I announced. "I'm tired of the cloud of suspicion that's hanging over you and Dina. It's time someone did something about it."

"And you think you're the one to do it?" Audie asked, shifting his gaze from the spot where he had been standing by the door.

"Why not?"

"Don't be stupid," Cord said. "It could be dangerous."

I stared at the two men. "I'm not some helpless Victorian maiden." I had to stop myself from stomping my foot. "Even if I'm dressed like one! I have a mind, and I intend to apply it to the question of Penn's murder."

"We don't know—" Audie started.

"Yes, murder," I repeated. "Premeditated and intentional. And I'm going to figure out who did it."

6

August 15, 1891
Dearest Mary,
*Last evening I visited with Ethan Hardy in
Oklahoma Town again. It was his wife Elizabeth's
time. He called for a doctor who has set up his practice
in town. As we waited through the long night hours,
I began to worry. A woman's lot is hard, and I want a
doctor near for you, dearest. I am sure they will plan for
more towns, as they did in the first land run. Should I
seek a plot of land in a town? It would be different than
the situation we considered with Ethan Hardy. I would
own my own business.*
*Elizabeth birthed a healthy baby boy. They are
calling him Benjamin Ethan Hardy.*
Your loving fiancé,
Robert Grace

Sunday, September 22

Audie's stony silence dampened my high spirits
even more than sitting in my rain-drenched clothes.
I struggled with buckling the seat belt over the

voluminous skirt while heat warmed the car and defogged the windows. Audie's Focus was a cozy and comfortable haven in spite of the miserable weather.

He put the gearshift into REVERSE and spun the car in a circle to head out of the driveway without speaking once. I decided to break the silence.

"What is it with men? Don't you think I'm capable of figuring out the angle a gun was fired? Or that I can do some investigating on my own?" I stared out the window as rain hit it in a splatter pattern. "Or am I supposed to mind my own business like a good ranch wife?"

"Cici!" My name exploded out of Audie's mouth like an epithet. "That's not the problem and you know it. I have no doubt that you can do whatever you set your mind to."

I knew that I wasn't being fair to Audie. He wasn't my father, the man who hoped, even counted on me to stay behind and help run the ranch while my sister abandoned us to pursue her dreams. He wasn't a local cowboy who expected me to prefer hot black coffee and sweet iced tea because that's the way things had always been. He didn't call my store my hobby instead of seeing it for what it was—a business and a chance to do something, be someone different. I adjusted the hat on my head, using the time to clear my mind of baggage that didn't belong to the man seated next to me.

"It's not your competence that I'm worried about," Audie continued in a calmer tone. "It's you—all of you. Someone has murdered once and thinks he got away with it."

"Or she," I pointed out.

"And *she*"—Audie emphasized the pronoun—"might kill again if she feels threatened. You could step on a hornets' nest without realizing it. 'A man cannot be too careful in the choice of his enemies.' " This time Audie quoted Wilde without his usual dash of humor. "You don't know who the enemy is. The killer probably feels safe as long as everyone thinks Penn's death was an accident."

I shook my head in frustration. Why didn't he understand? "But as long as everyone thinks Penn's death was a dreadful accident, blame will fall on either Dina or Cord. Or both of them. No. I refuse to let that happen as long as I can do something about it."

Audie pounded his hands against the steering wheel. The car jerked and skidded over the slick road. He took a deep breath and brought the vehicle back under control. "I can't jump a horse over a fence, but I can put my body in front of yours if anything happens. And I may need to if you insist on looking into the murder."

Wow. Both Cord and Audie had expressed concern about my safety, like two roosters fighting over the right to protect me. I only hoped that no one got hurt in the process, including me. I put my hand on Audie's arm.

"You really are a noble friend," I said. His eyes slanted a question at me. "Audwin. I looked up your name on the Internet one day to find its meaning." I blushed as I said this. Fathers didn't name their boys Audwin in Oklahoma, and I was curious. "Audwin means noble friend, and it describes you well."

Audie huffed. "I hope to be more than your *friend*. Once you get over this obsession with the murder." Once again, I was reminded of a rooster crowing.

"It's a place to start." I smiled at him, and he smiled back. Something inside of me pinged, like a chord not plucked for a long time.

Audie smirked, as if he had won the first round of the cock fight. His voice turned serious. "You can at least wait until the police get the ballistics report. There is no need to go around stirring up trouble if the tests prove it was—well, an accident, you know."

"No, no," I said. "If someone exchanged real bullets for the blanks, then it was someone besides Dina. She takes good care of the props. You know that. You've worked with her before."

Audie grinned at the memory. I bet he hadn't known what to do with the green-haired teenager who arrived at the theater for the first open audition and announced her desire to manage the props. No one else expressed interest—they all wanted a part in the play—and she had experience with a couple of high school productions. She won the position by default. After that, she twisted my arm for assistance with costumes and introduced me to Audie.

"I've never regretted my decision to take her on," Audie admitted. "There's never been a single missing prop, not even at a rehearsal. She was extra careful with those guns."

"Think about Cord's theory for a minute. It makes sense. Anyone familiar with the story of the gunfight would know when to shoot. The exchange of gunfire would cover the sound; and no one would be looking their way because everyone's attention was on Cord and Penn. 'Nothing captures an audience like a good fight.' Isn't that what you said?"

"You would throw my words back at me." Audie grimaced. He had instructed his actors to make their stage fight realistic. "But surely someone would notice somebody with a rifle. Someone besides Penn or Cord, of course."

"All kinds of people were carrying around rifles yesterday. Men, women. Even the children had pop guns. I think it made them feel like real pioneers, like those statues of frontier women in Ponca City."

"Carrying a weapon isn't the same as firing it. They were taking an awful risk, aiming a rifle in plain sight. That saloon front had no windows."

"It could have been a revolver. It probably was." Why was Audie being so stubborn about it? "The art of misdirection at the opportune moment."

Audie snorted. "That's it, then. All we need to do is find a magician with a reason to kill Penn. Were there any wandering minstrels in the crowd yesterday?"

"Like your mime act?" I had to laugh at that. Audie had arranged for clowns to entertain the children with balloons and magic tricks.

"Your theory has one additional advantage." Audie's voice came out strangely, as if the words strangled his throat.

"What's that?"

"It clears Cord from suspicion."

"You don't really think Cord did it?"

"No. But maybe I wish he did."

Oh. The heart of the matter, the rooster wanting any advantage over his opponent. The second round went to Cord by default.

We didn't say much more until we arrived at my father's house at the Crazy W Ranch. Crazy and wild, that described my family's name and heritage. As soon as Audie parked his Focus, Jenna dashed out.

"Oh, good, you're here. I need you to go to the store." Jenna didn't wait for a response. "Here's the shopping list. Dina didn't have *any* of the things I need to make my special California salad. Organic, if possible. Dad has the chicken on the grill."

Audie looked at the still gray sky. Only Jenna would plan to grill outside on a rainy day. New Mexico had spoiled her. Maybe there they could cook outside year round. I didn't really know.

"Of course it took quite a bit of effort to get the grill onto the porch, but it's done, and then I discovered we didn't have any avocados or fresh oranges and apricots. I did find prunes." She giggled. "Go on. I still have to cut up the potatoes for French fries." At least my sister hadn't become a total health nut, as long as she still made French fries from potatoes grown in our own garden, a Wilde family favorite.

"And hurry, will you? Dad and Dina are famished. I don't know why, after that *enormous* lunch everyone had at church." Jenna dashed inside.

"I'm sorry," I said to Audie. "Do you mind? My sister is a force of nature."

"So I see." Audie looked shell-shocked, the way

most people did when the winds of Hurricane Jenna passed over them. "No, of course not." He backed the car up and turned around, heading down the short distance of our driveway. The Crazy W ranch hadn't expanded as much as the Circle G had, and our farmhouse sat close to the road.

I studied Audie's profile. The rain had ruffled his careful hairstyle so that it lay in unorganized strands around his head. It was rather darling, showing the shape of his skull to good advantage. I wondered if he had ever shaved it all off. People did that in the city, I heard, although here in Oklahoma we would probably think "Nazis" and "skinheads," and any boy who shaved his head would receive a whipping from his father. I guessed that Audie always wore his hair long, in the style of artists the world over. He would look good either way.

"I'm sorry about today," I said. "Not exactly the kind of day we planned." When Audie invited me to the concert, I expected a day of worship and music followed by a quiet family dinner. Instead, he saw his date dancing the cancan on stage and then endured a long chat with his rival about the repercussions of Penn's death.

"None of it is your fault." Audie's shoulders relaxed a fraction. "No one expected Penn to die. And I will help you in any way I can."

I knew he still didn't agree with my desire to pursue the murderer, which made his offer even sweeter. The car ate up the miles into town.

"Which store?" Audie asked as we reached the edge of the business district.

I looked at Jenna's shopping list. "The Shop 'n' Save. They have the best produce." I had no idea which store carried organic goods, and I didn't care. I wanted juicy, plump fruit, regardless of how it was grown.

We entered the store and headed down the produce aisle. I grabbed a bag of mixed salad greens instead of the requested iceberg and romaine lettuce. That would have to suffice. I studied the shopping list again, automatically alphabetizing the items: almonds, apple, avocado, apricot, celery, olive oil, orange. "Why not call it the A-plus salad." I giggled at my own joke.

Audie looked at the list. "Add an artichoke. And asparagus."

I pretended to gag. "Or how about this? It's called araza." I held up a round, yellow fruit. "I think I will."

"Tell me about Jenna. The two of you seem so different." Audie stopped at the apple bins. "Which type do you think she wants? They taste so different."

I studied the varieties, the faithful red delicious, and softer Jonathans, and my gaze hit upon an *A*. "Let's try the Ariane." I dropped a couple of apples into a bag and twisted the top.

Jenna. The orange that grew on the Wilde family apple tree. We rarely talked about Jenna's past, although we didn't make a secret of it. Anyone who lived in Grace Gulch twenty years ago knew the truth. I saw no harm in telling Audie the story, and it might help him understand the Wilde family dynamics better.

"Jenna's always been a bit wild."

"From birth," Audie replied solemnly. "So have you." Then he grinned to let me know it was a joke.

"Oh, you know what I mean. She's six years older than me. When I was a kid, it seemed like she was determined to break every rule Mom and Dad set down."

We left the produce section in search of slivered almonds and salad dressings.

"When Jenna was fifteen, she became pregnant." I said it matter-of-factly. At nine, I relished the idea of another baby in the family. The shame and despair that engulfed my mother at the time had washed over me without leaving a trace.

"Mom and Dad decided to keep her child and raise her as their own. A couple of months after I turned ten, just two weeks shy of Jenna's sixteenth birthday, she gave birth to a baby girl."

"Dina." Audie understood immediately.

"Dina, yes. She's my niece by birth and my sister by adoption."

"That helps me understand why she's so different from you. I thought it was probably because she's the baby of the family."

The next aisle over, we stopped in front of the salad dressings. "I confess I'm not fond of olive oil."

Audie grabbed a bottle of Catalina dressing. "I've had this on fruit salads. It's pretty good." He added olive oil. "For Jenna's sake."

"Dad handled Jenna's wild streak better than Mom.

She never seemed to recover from the shock. She died unexpectly, a couple of weeks before Jenna graduated from high school." The remembered pain of those days made my eyes sting. "Then Jenna left for college in the fall and never came back. To live here, I mean."

"You must have been lonely."

I appreciated that about Audie. He understood unspoken things. We grabbed a bag of almonds and headed for the checkout. We continued talking while the clerk weighed each bag of fruit.

"With Mom dead and Jenna gone, I took over with Dina. After high school, I stayed in town and went to Grace Gulch Community College for two years. The same school Dina is attending now." Our community college attracted people from across Lincoln County.

"Didn't you graduate from some fashion design school in Houston?"

I nodded. "I crammed my junior and senior years into three semesters and graduated early. It was wonderful. Then I came back home."

I paid the cashier. Audie grabbed the bags and headed out to the car. I followed, continuing the story.

"To give her credit, Jenna has always supported Dina, even when she was in college. And Dina's always known the truth. But when Jenna comes home, it's like I don't exist."

"Like the father visiting his kids every other weekend. Party time."

"Exactly." I swallowed past the lump in my throat. It was foolish to harbor anger at my elder sister. "Dina gets into trouble with this shooting, and there's Jenna, swooping in to rescue her. Even if she had already planned to come for Land Run Days." Why hadn't Dina come to me with her troubles?

The rain had stopped, leaving the early evening sky crisp and clear. Audie stuffed the bags in the trunk of the car and put his arms around me.

"Oh, Cici. You don't have to prove anything. To Dina. Or to me."

I felt safe and secure in the circle of his arms. Safe enough to cry. So I did. Audie didn't say anything. He rubbed my back and let me cry, my tears soaking the front of his shirt more surely than the afternoon's rainstorm. Eventually I stopped. I lifted my face to his and looked into those beautiful blue eyes. He leaned down and kissed me, once, lightly, on the lips. Then he dug in the pocket of his jeans and dabbed a monogrammed handkerchief on my face, wiping away the traces of tears.

"I would kiss away every tear," he said. "But then we might be here all night." He managed a weak smile and stepped back. "Are you okay?"

His words broke the wonder of the moment. "I'm fine now." My voice didn't quiver, and I opened the passenger door to prove my point. "We'd better get going, before they send the posse after us."

A few minutes later, we were back at the house. Jenna and Dina worked in the kitchen, cubing the chicken. Cool, damp air carried spicy aromas from the grill into the house. Jenna raised an eyebrow at our odd assortment of fruits and vegetables but didn't comment. Audie took on the task of chopping the araza for the salad. He handed each of us a piece to try. It tasted a bit like banana.

"We decided to create our own recipe," I explained, stirring the fruit into the mix. "It's a California A-plus Salad."

Dina giggled.

"I like it." Jenna shook olive oil and lemon juice in a cruet but left the Catalina dressing in the bottle. "No need to be fancy." She did the honors of tossing the ingredients together in a huge ceramic bowl that she sent us from New Mexico one Christmas. Made by Native Americans, of course. I reminded her that Oklahoma prided itself on its Indian heritage. She had retorted that the Navajo and Apache cultures were very different.

Before long we sat in our comfortable kitchen, the window open to let in the rain-cleansed air, mismatched silverware adding a family touch to the table. Dad stared at the fruit salad, searching his extensive bank of memorized proverbs for an appropriate quote. " 'The fruit of the righteous is a tree of life.' "

"Proverbs 11:30. I love the end of that verse. 'And he who wins souls is wise.' " Audie could match Dad, verse for verse.

Dad beamed. "Will you say the blessing, Audie?"

Audie spoke a brief prayer, and we passed the salad.

"You two disappeared after the concert," Jenna

said. "People wanted to get a picture of us, the three Wilde sisters together."

"Yeah. Maybe we could have used it as a publicity photo and gone on tour." Dina giggled.

I bit off the response to the outrageous suggestion that sat on the tip of my tongue. I knew Dina was joking. "We had to make a stop." I saw no need to explain the conversation we had overheard between Chief Reiner and Cord. Audie took his cue from me and didn't expand on my explanation.

Jenna took a bite of the improvised salad. "Mmm, perfect. You'll have to tell me the name of that fruit again. This is even better than my standard California salad recipe."

Dina heaped her plate full with salad and crisp French fries and her own specialty, flaky biscuits. She must have been hungry after her appetite-deprived lunch. We addressed ourselves to enjoying the meal.

"Officer Waller asked me to come to the police station again in the morning," Dina said after she ate the last bite of biscuit and pushed back her plate. "Why do they want to talk with me again? I've already told them everything I know." She glanced at me. "And before you say anything, I've asked our lawyer to go with me."

Uh-oh. Audie and I exchanged glances. "We might know something about that. We ran into the police after the concert."

"They said you made a threat against Penn when he turned you down for an internship at the *Herald*,"

Audie said bluntly. "And Cici says it's true."

"What threat?" Dina thought for a moment and her face reddened. "But. . ." She spluttered. "I didn't mean anything by it. I mean, I got a job at the *Sequoian* instead, and it's much better. Mr. Gaynor lets me do a lot more things."

Five forks poised in midair over partially eaten salads. Three pairs of eyes stared accusingly at Audie, then me.

"Not to worry." Audie grinned. "If people committed murder every time they lost a gig, I'd be a murderer several times over."

7

August 30, 1891
Dearest Mary,

I am thankful for your godly advice. We must trust God to protect us and our land, after He guides us to the place He has chosen for us. Pardon my loving concern. I continue to seek the perfect place, and I believe I have found it.

I rode out in the Sac and Fox Nation yesterday. Patches crested a hill and a piece of Eden spread out before me. A clear river cuts through the center of a verdant valley. The soil is a rich red clay, and every kind of tree grows on the river banks. Your peach and apple orchards will thrive. Small game of rabbits and squirrel abound. It is not quite a valley, more of a gulch, really, nestled between two hills.

God willing, the land will be included in the next run.
Your loving fiancé,
Robert Grace

Sunday, September 22

Lost a gig? Murder? The idea was so ridiculous that I joined the others in relieved laughter. Trust Audie to know the right thing to say.

"That's why I like being my own boss." Maybe I was babbling. I was trying to reassure my younger sister that I understood her feelings. I called Dina "sister" for convenience. I would do anything to protect the dear girl, even if she was now a grown-up nineteen and proud of the fact. But Audie's comments diverted my attention. He had opened a door to his past—something he rarely did—and I wanted to find out more. "So you've lost a lot of gigs?" I waggled my eyebrows at Audie. "Do tell."

"It's the nature of acting." Audie took the last bite of meat and crossed his knife and fork on his plate. "No one has a job for life."

"He's being overly modest." Dina took a biscuit and buttered it. "Mrs. Mallory told us all about him when she introduced him to the cast. Plays, commercials, even some films. You were pretty much a bigwig in Chicago." She shook her finger at Audie.

"Well, I had some success." A blush spread across his pale cheeks.

"I want to hear all about it." Dad's voice swung between interested host and a father interrogating a teenage boy on his daughter's first date. "But first I want a slice of pecan pie."

Every year we spent hours shelling twenty pounds of nuts from the pecan harvest which Dina turned into delicious pies and toppings and cakes. She surprised us all by taking home economics and becoming the best baker in the family. I poured cups of coffee—nothing goes better with dessert than hot, black coffee—and we retired to the living room, bringing the coffeepot with us. "Who wants ice cream with the pie?" I asked. Audie and Jenna said yes. Although she bought organic vegetables when possible, Jenna liked her comfort foods.

I wondered how our lived-in parlor looked to a sophisticated man like Audie. Our sleeper sofa, bought for Jenna's occasional trips home while she attended college, sagged at one end. Before I could warn Audie about the spring he should avoid, our dog and cat jumped into place and curled together. Ralphie the dog slept there every chance he got, and his weight had pressed it down over the years as his bulk increased. Jenna plopped down next to the animals. She crooned over them and scratched the pony-sized dog under his chin.

I poured myself a fresh cup of coffee and rejoined Audie on the loveseat. My scheming sisters made sure the seating turned out that way. I was pleased that Jenna hadn't claimed the spot.

From her place at the corner of the couch, Dina leaned forward, deep in discussion with Audie. She wanted to know every detail of his time with the Chicago Shakespeare Theater troupe.

"Why Shakespeare?" I asked. "Wasn't there a company devoted to Oscar Wilde?"

Audie laughed. "Unfortunately, no. Maybe I should have started one. But by the time the CST offered me a position, I'd had enough of waiting tables and doing the odd play every now and then. I appreciated the steady work."

"Tell us about the films Mrs. Mallory mentioned," Dina said.

"I was a bit actor in a couple of tragedies. Blink, and you'd miss me."

"Oh? Which ones?" I asked. I would never admit that the only Shakespeare films I had seen were *A Midsummer Night's Dream* with a young Mickey Rooney and the 1960s version of *Romeo and Juliet* that every high school freshman watched.

"*King Lear. Merchant of Venice.* That's the extent of my film career."

A lot of aspiring actors would love to have even that much.

"So what made you decide to leave fame and fortune for rural Oklahoma?" Dad asked the question that had occupied my mind ever since Audie's arrival in our town. I had heard his practiced answer—"I felt that it was time for a change"—but it still puzzled me, and I wanted to know more.

"I realized that I was never going to win an Oscar or an Emmy or a Tony, and I didn't like the person I was becoming in pursuit of fame. I was afraid that I was making theater my god." Audie stood up and poured himself a fresh cup of coffee. "I thought about giving up the theater altogether. But I couldn't seem to let it go. Like Wilde, 'I love acting. It is so much more real than life.' " His face twisted in a smile.

"I'm so glad you stuck with it!" Dina tucked her leg under her. "You're so *good* at what you do. It's a God-given gift."

Be quiet. I wanted Audie to continue sharing his heart.

He obliged. "I still hadn't decided when I went on

a missions trip with my church's youth group. I helped them do mimes and puppet shows and stuff like that. Everywhere we went, people gathered. God reminded me that there is a whole world of theater outside of the cities. Like any art form, theater isn't bad by itself. The question was how God wanted me to use the gifts He had given me."

Audie's insight touched me. "Like fashion." I waved at my outfit for the day. "Fashions come and go. There is nothing wrong in wanting to look your best. But when you spend too much money on it, or worry too much about it. . ." I stopped, embarrassment overtaking my enthusiasm.

"Exactly." The smile Audie turned in my direction made my worries float away. "I asked God what He wanted me to do with theater—if anything. Large parts of the country are hungry for live theater. I felt God was calling me to do something about it." He paused and moderated his excited tones. "So I put my name out there. When Magda contacted me about becoming director at the MGM, I jumped at the opportunity."

Magda Grace Mallory is Grace Gulch's biggest supporter of the arts. I'd heard rumors of a proposed fine arts complex. For now she supported a music center where kids from nine to ninety-two could study. Today's pit orchestra resulted from that effort. The benefits trickled down to high school; our marching band won more competitions than the football team they supported.

But theater was Mrs. Mallory's first love. She managed the community theater for years. After she bought the old Grace Gulch Orpheum and rechristened it the Magda Grace Mallory Theater, she decided to look for a professional replacement. Audie accepted the position on a year's trial basis. I was holding my breath, hoping he would decide to make Grace Gulch his permanent home.

"And nothing has happened to make me regret my decision." Audie looked straight at me. "In fact, I think it's the best choice I've ever made."

Heat rushed to my cheeks, and I looked at the floor to hide the telltale blush. Like a tracker in hunting season, he was pursuing me with persistence and considerable charm. No wonder I found him irresistible. If only he decided to stay—

"Not even death at high noon?" Jenna wiggled her eyebrows in that exaggerated way of hers.

I held my breath. Audie laughed. "Not even that. I confess that I expected Grace Gulch to be crime free."

Dina snickered. She read the local police blotter with avid interest. Like any other town, Grace Gulch had its share of drunks and petty theft. She told me about a few of her own harmless pranks from her last year in high school. After the fact, of course. Mayor Ron still wondered who had papered the cedar tree in his front yard on New Year's Eve. But I thought I knew what Audie meant: free of major crimes, not minor misdemeanors.

"Murders were a dime a dozen in Chicago. They didn't even rate prime time coverage unless someone notable was involved." Audie's face sobered. "I never had a front row seat before. I never knew the victim."

No one seemed to know how to respond.

Dad retired to bed shortly after that, and Audie and I said good-bye to Dina and Jenna. With the energy snapping between them, I knew that they would spend the hours until dawn in an all-night gab fest. I almost wanted to stay. I was as wired as they were, given everything that had happened.

"Good night, you two," Jenna called after us. "Don't do anything I wouldn't do." Her laughter followed us out into the hallway.

Audie retrieved my cape from the coat rack near the front door and draped it over my shoulders. He descended the front steps first, then held out his hand to steady my arm. I felt like a lady of a hundred years ago, a rare, precious thing that triggered a man's desire to protect. He kept up the charade by opening the car door, and then closing it after I settled in the seat. Chariots come in many makes and sizes, and this particular model was quite comfortable.

A few minutes later Audie pulled up in front of my house. The afternoon rain left the sky crystal clear, every star a pinpoint of light in the black box of the sky. I looked at the familiar constellations. "Look at that." I sighed. "What is it that Job says? Something about bringing out the bear with her cubs?"

"I'd rather look at you."

I felt his gaze on my face and turned toward him. The pale light suited him, shadows making peaks and valleys of his features. His eyes looked darker. Was it a trick of the light? Then he leaned forward, and I forgot about the stars.

Our lips brushed once, and then again. Light

exploded within me, fireworks worthy of the Fourth of July, not a chilly September evening. Then Audie pulled back, and darkness descended. He smiled, a dear half smile, and ran a thumb across my mouth. "You have unexpected fire inside of you, Miss Wilde."

He walked me to my door and waited until I went inside. I heard his feet traipsing down the front steps. A wave of light-headedness washed over me, and I leaned against the doorjamb, feeling like a schoolgirl with her first crush instead of a responsible, twenty-nine going on forever businesswoman. A cool breeze wafted through the screen door and brought me to my senses. Like it or not, it was time for bed. While I undressed, I studied my garments. The blouse shirtwaist needed drycleaning, but the skirt could go another day once I brushed off the mud from the hem. For tomorrow I planned on wearing a cadet blue velvet walking dress with a tiered hemline that allowed my legs to move freely, and a hip-hugging jacket adorned with white piping. It always made me feel attractive.

I went through the motions of my nightly routine, although I decided against brushing my hair one hundred strokes. My hair stuck out at odd angles after the rain. The only cure was a deep conditioning after the next shampoo. I grabbed my Bible and read a few verses, and then prayed about everything that had happened. Once again I asked that I would not be jealous of the relationship between Jenna and Dina. The hands on the clock skipped over midnight, but I couldn't settle down to sleep. Thoughts of Audie, the suspicions thrown on Cord and Dina, Jenna's reappearance in our lives, and Cord's theories about the gunshot fought for priority in my head. For a few minutes I focused on the murder, seeking ways to salvage Dina's reputation. That was the most important thing, wasn't it? But my rebellious thoughts wandered back to Audie. How long would a talented and experienced actor remain in little old Grace Gulch? Was I in danger of losing my heart to a man who would move on to greener pastures before long? I remembered his comments on seeking God's will and tried to leave my worries in the Almighty's hands. After that, sleep came quickly.

The few hours of sleep that I managed refreshed me more than expected. I woke with renewed purpose and with a clear idea of my plans for the day. I wanted to bask in memories of Audie's kiss, but I needed to find out who was in front of the Gulch at the time of the gunfight. I started coffee brewing and dialed Dina's cell phone.

She answered on the second ring. "Hey, sis. What's up?" Energy bounced through her words as if she had been up for hours. Perhaps she had. In fact, she might never have gone to bed. Ah, to have that kind of stamina!

I cleared my throat. "I have a question. You were in the Gulch just before the shooting, right?"

"Yeah. I went outside when Cord and Mr. Hardy galloped by."

"Do you remember who else was there?" I held my breath. Dina often focused on a single object to the exclusion of everything else. Her interest in the play might have blinded her to anything going on around her.

"Let me think." I imagined her wrinkling her forehead under her impossibly red hair. "Mitch was there, taking pictures for the *Sequoian*. Mrs. Hardy was there, bragging about her husband's part in the play." Her voice turned sad. "Poor Mrs. Hardy. How awful for her."

That was another item to add to my to-do list. Visit Penn Hardy's widow, Gwen.

"And Mayor Ron was there, of course, carrying on like the reenactment was his idea." She giggled. "At least one good thing came out of the shooting."

What on earth?

"We were spared the mayor's speech," Dina said.

Laughter replaced the reprimand that came to my lips. Mayor Ron Grace spoke at every public gathering, often weaving something about the great legacy of the Grace family into his address. To hear him tell it, his family took credit for every hamlet and city that had the name of Grace in it. Most of the time, I tuned out his braggadocio.

"I'm sorry, that's all I remember," Dina concluded. "I gotta go. I'm supposed to be at work in twenty minutes."

I looked at the list of names she had given me. Mitch Gaynor, Gwen Hardy, Ron Grace. It was a start. Maybe my customers today would remember more.

Time to get ready for work. I checked my reflection in the mirror and decided I needed to wash my hair. I didn't relish the prospect; no matter what brand of expensive shampoo I used, or how often I applied conditioner, my hair remained a frizzled, dry mess. Nevertheless, I climbed in the shower, lathered my hair twice, and left on a conditioner that smelled like strawberries and champagne according to the bottle, while I bathed my body. I blow-dried my hair into submission, pulling it into a severe bun. The process took an hour. After that I read my Bible while I had a cup of coffee and a bowl of oatmeal. At twenty-five minutes past nine, I left for the store.

I parked in an alley behind the store and walked around to the front of the building. Seeing the words Cici's Vintage Clothing etched into the glass with Antigua lettering always brought a smile to my face. It represented a dream come true, proof that I could do something besides be a rancher's wife. I took a hand-kerchief from my purse and rubbed at a small spot on the glass then unlocked the front door. I didn't turn the sign to OPEN yet; I wanted to check the displays and open the registers first.

I started coffee brewing and poured tea over a pitcher of ice. Later today I would stop by Gaynor Goodies for fresh cookies; Saturday's leftovers had become as hard as week-old doughnuts over the weekend. I made a point of providing refreshments. They encouraged clients to spend more time in my store, and the extra sales more than compensated for the occasional spill.

A soft knock reminded me that I hadn't unlocked the front door yet. I turned the sign to OPEN and greeted a friend from high school.

"Cici!" The now city lawyer and former high

school cheerleader rushed into the store with the same enthusiasm she used waving pom-poms. Two ladies followed her in. "I've been telling my friends about your wonderful store, and while we were here for Land Run Days, we just had to check it out."

The day had begun.

Business was brisk for a Monday morning. More people had remained in town past the weekend than I had expected. With each sale I rang up, I gave the customer my business card with my Web site address and asked, "Were you here for the festivities this weekend?" Most people told me how much they enjoyed the weekend, especially the reenactment, until that awful accident on Saturday. I wasted some time answering their questions, but fortunately the out-of-town guests didn't seem to realize I had rushed to Cord's side. From there it was easy to ask who else they saw watching the gunfight.

My lawyer friend identified Dina. "That was your sister, wasn't it, with that Santa red hair? I couldn't help noticing her. Most of the time I was watching the action as closely as if I were going to be called as a witness at Cord's trial." She raised a hand at my shocked look. "Or should I say Bob Grace's trial? I was thinking of the original feud. I didn't notice much else."

Many people, strangers to town, mentioned the girl with the red hair. I wondered if my sister knew how noticeable she was. She probably did and welcomed the attention. You didn't dye your hair every color of the rainbow if you wanted to stay anonymous.

Visitors who had stopped by the Gulch for

refreshments mentioned Suzanne. They described the actress as "that lady with the big hairdo, who looked right at home." Suzanne Jay could certainly dance the cancan like a professional saloon worker. Apparently she came to the swinging doors and watched the action along with everyone else.

I had better luck when Enid Waldberg came into the store about eleven with a couple of ladies from church. A month ago, Enid had admired my prairie bonnets, commenting how practical they were for protecting your head from the sun. She loved to garden but had to slather on sun screen; her Scandinavian skin burned easily. She had studied every bonnet I had in stock and then left without buying any.

"Cici!" She gathered me in an obligatory hug. I loved our pastor's wife. We all did; her sweet nature complemented her husband's forceful personality perfectly.

"How are you doing?" Enid looked at me as if she knew every feeling I had suffered for the past three days and every doubt that had been cast on my family. Come to think of it, she probably did know the gossip. The rumor mill thrived in Grace Gulch. In another time or place, I would have been glad to talk things over with her. Today, however, I had questions to ask and a store to run.

"I'm doing okay." I wondered if she came in just to chat or to do some real shopping.

"Do you have anything on sale?" one of the church ladies asked. "We thought you might mark down some items after the festival."

Ah, a bargain hunter. I recognized the breed,

people who didn't understand the cost of locating, restoring, or recreating period costumes.

"Not yet," I said brightly. In fact, I wondered if my stock would last through the week. "Enid, I have something to show you."

She followed me to my back office, and I handed her a slim white box. "This is for you." When she hesitated, I said, "Go ahead, open it."

When she failed to buy a bonnet, I decided to surprise her with one. I had chosen a pale blue calico, with sprigs of white and purple lilacs. "Try it on."

"Oh, my." Her trembling fingers settled the bonnet on her head and tied the strings beneath her chin. She studied her reflection in a small wall mirror, turning her head from side to side. "It's gorgeous. You shouldn't have." She removed it and folded it back into the box.

"It's my pleasure." I beamed. "I only wish that I had given it to you before Land Run Days. What did you think of the play?"

"Audie did a magnificent job staging it, didn't he? It was wonderful, except for the awful tragedy, of course."

"This may sound strange, but did you notice who was standing in front of the Gulch?"

Enid didn't ask why I wanted to know. She closed her eyes as if to envision the scene. "Dina. Suzanne Jay."

My heart plummetted. I hoped she had noticed someone new that no one else had mentioned yet.

"Mitch Gaynor. Mayor Grace. Gwen Hardy." She thought longer and mentioned more names. "I was

there with my husband and a few others from church."
She opened her eyes. "Those are the only people I
remember. Is it important?"

"It might be."

"I'll ask the ladies and let you know what I find
out."

I made a pencil sketch of the sidewalk in front of
the Gulch and asked her to mark where everyone was
standing. Her memory put mine to shame. I could
take note of what attracted people in my store, as well
as which items they passed on. But in other places, I
didn't pay as close attention.

The trio departed the store without purchasing
anything. Half an hour later, the phone rang. "I've
checked around," Enid said without preamble. "The
people I mentioned are the only ones anyone remembers
seeing near the door to the Gulch."

If Cord's theory about the direction of the gunfire
was correct, I had my list of suspects.

8

September 10, 1891
Dearest Mary,
Another man has discovered the dale which I have begun to think of as our own. I returned there today, considering where we could build our cabin, plant a garden, and dig a well. I pictured enjoying a picnic with you under a spreading elm tree.

Then while I was enjoying a drink of cool river water in the shade of a tree, a stranger approached. He rode among the trees much as I had on my first visit, testing the leaves for fullness of life. I could tell he was assessing the land. I confess I had hoped that God would hide this spot from the eyes of other land seekers.

The stranger heard the noise and turned in my direction. He introduced himself as Dick Gaynor. I expect he didn't like finding me there any more than I liked finding him.
Your loving fiancé,
Robert Grace

———

Monday, September 23
In between customers, I studied Enid's sketch of

the front of the Gulch. None of the people listed struck me as likely killers, and I couldn't imagine how any of them could fire a gun unseen. That was the problem. I couldn't visualize the angles. But I knew someone who could: Audie. He had to do it every time he designed a stage set.

I dialed his cell.

"Cici! It's good to hear from you today." His silky voice tickled my ear, intimate beyond mere friendship.

The sound teased memories of last night's kiss to the forefront of my mind. The morning's information gathering had pushed it into the background. The sparks the kiss had created last night now flamed into fire and spread across my face, and in the confusion I blurted out my request. "Can you join me for lunch?"

"I'd love to. Where shall we meet?"

"The Gulch."

Silence on the other end. When Audie spoke again, his silky tones had turned to business casual. "This isn't a social call, is it?"

"Maybe it is. Can't it be both a social call and a business call?" The words coming out of my mouth surprised me. I wasn't the flirting type. I hoped my hurried invitation hadn't diminished whatever grew between us. Then again, if a simple request between friends could ruin a romance, then Audie wasn't the man I thought he was.

"I'll be there in ten minutes." Audie disconnected the line.

I fought the impulse to cry.

Two customers came in and bought vintage purses

before I could change my store sign to CLOSED and lock the front door. I moved the hands on the WILL RETURN AT sign to quarter past two o'clock. Our discussion might take awhile. Audie waved at me from across the street, and I hurried to meet him.

"What's up?" he asked as we walked into the Gulch. Although the false saloon front was still in place, they had reverted to their usual menu and regular staff. Suzanne of the bouffant hair had disappeared back to the theater.

"Let's get some lunch first," I said. "I'm hungry." I knew what I wanted without consulting the menu. Audie took his time perusing the selections and decided on biscuits and gravy—"The best-kept secret of Oklahoma cooking," he called it—with fresh coffee.

While we waited for the food, I showed Audie my sketch. "I'm pretty sure that these are all the people who were in front of the Gulch during the gunfight."

"The people who could have taken a shot, you mean." Audie pushed pale bangs away from his eyes while he examined the crosses and circles on the paper, turning it in his hands as if to get different perspectives.

"I know it's not very clear. I thought you could make another sketch. You know, like staging a scene for a play. Think of it in terms of entrances and exits."

"Exit, stage left," Audie murmured. His pen poised over a soft paper napkin.

"Here, I've got something better." I dug a pad of lined paper from my purse.

"Thanks." He looked at the sketch. "Where are the

saloon doors?" He sketched out the main street, the street in the front center, vanishing into the west in the distance. The waitress arrived with our food. Audie tore the sheet of paper off the pad and folded it in half.

Neither one of us spoke until we took a bite of our food. I savored the flavor of the chicken salad on my tongue. Audie forked his biscuits with the enthusiasm of a toddler discovering a new food.

At last Audie leaned back and reached for his napkin. "You know that I don't like the idea of you looking into the shooting. It's dangerous."

How sweet. He wanted to protect me from the big bad wolf instead of expecting me to grab a gun and help hunt it down. And how outdated. I was a twenty-first century woman—even if I did dress in clothes more than a hundred years old.

"Nothing's going to happen to me," I said. *But what about you?* What if something happened to Audie because he helped me? Worry was a two-way street.

"Oh, I expect that something's going to happen to you all right." Amused fire danced in his darkened eyes. "Something even more adventurous than chasing down a murderer."

I choked on a chunk of celery. "You sound sure of yourself."

He glanced away and when he looked back, the fire in his eyes had died out and his eyes had returned to their usual sapphire blue. "No, not sure of myself. Just sure of what I want." He smiled. "Dessert? Would you like to share a cookies-and-cream milkshake?"

A milkshake? Drink out of two straws over a

single glass? Stare into Audie's mesmerizing eyes? *Live dangerously*, I decided.

"Why not?"

When the waitress returned with the milkshake a few minutes later, Audie put his hand over mine. Leaning forward to take the straw between my lips, I stared into eyes that reflected my own dreams and hopes and aspirations. For a moment I let myself believe.

The waitress placed our check on the table without speaking, but her appearance broke the dreamlike trance. News of this very public display would reach all of downtown within the hour, and Cord's ears by suppertime.

The thought of Cord undid the magic, and I withdrew my hand from Audie's. Did I like Audie enough, know him well enough, to hurt Cord that way? To cover my confusion, I studied the unfinished drawing. "Do you need me to tell you where everyone was standing?"

Audie swallowed the last of the shake and sighed. Regret flickered in his eyes, but when he spoke, he returned to the business at hand. "Why don't you show me? Outside." We paid the bill, and I insisted on splitting it, since I had invited him to lunch.

We exited through the swinging doors, and I got into position. "Suzanne was standing here."

Audie marked it on his sketch.

I moved a few feet to the right, beside the pole that held up one side of the overhanging roof. "Dina was here. And Pastor Waldberg and Enid were standing over there." I pointed to the pole on the left side of the roof.

"In what order? Was anyone standing in front of someone else?"

I consulted the notes Enid had given me. "The pastor was in back, with one of the husbands. The three ladies stood in front of the men."

As Audie continued to take notes, I said, "Mayor Ron stayed right smack in front of the doors. Enid said she heard Suzanne asking him to move so she could see better. She came out herself a bit later."

"Who was between the Waldbergs and the mayor?"

"Maybe half a dozen people, mostly from out of town. I don't know their names."

"How about between Dina and the mayor?" Audie didn't remove his gaze from the sketch.

"Not as many people." I checked my list. "Gwen Hardy. Mitch Gaynor. Young Sammy Hardy." I went on to name a few others.

Audie handed me the sketch. I glanced at it and a thought struck me. "Would you do one more thing for me?"

"Sure," he said as I glanced up and down the street.

No cars in sight. "Go out into the street, about where Penn fell down."

He checked for oncoming traffic, and then walked into the street with a bit of a cowboy's swagger. He spread his arms as if to say, "Here I am."

I walked over to the left side of the sidewalk, where the Waldbergs stood, and pretended to aim a gun. I couldn't find a spot where I could get a clear view of Audie's chest. A hot dog stand put up for the weekend's festivities blocked the view.

Audie dashed to safety when a couple of cars passed and then returned to his position. With a sinking heart, I walked to the left side of the Gulch. I put myself in Mayor Ron's place. Check. Suzanne Jay. Check. Mitch Gaynor. Check. Gwen Hardy. Check. Last of all—Dina. Any one of them had a clear view of Penn. So far my investigaton had accomplished nothing but to prove my sister could have killed Penn.

Another car sped past, and Audie jumped back.

"I'm done." There was no need for Audie to endanger himself anymore.

"What's the matter?" Audie stared at the sketch I held in my hands, as if seeking to piece together the puzzle that had me stumped.

"It's one of them." I pointed to the group to the left of the saloon door.

Audie sucked in his breath when he saw my finger pointed at Dina's name. "Cici." This time his silky voice wrapped itself around my wounded heart and soothed the fear that crouched there, ready to spring into full-fledged panic.

"This isn't any good. I need to talk with everybody who was in a position to make the shot."

"Not without me! You have to promise to let me tag along."

I smiled wearily. "I promise. But now I have to get back to work." I checked my watch to confirm the time. A few minutes past two. "Why don't we plan on paying a call on Mrs. Hardy after I close up shop today?"

Audie agreed. He leaned close as if to give me a kiss, but my face must have given me away. *Not here. Not now.* He smiled and said good-bye.

Jenna parked in front of my store as I crossed the street. "I hear you had quite a lunch with your actor friend." She smirked at me while I unlocked the door.

"How did *you* hear about it?"

"Oh, the grapevine is alive and well."

This was even worse than I had feared, if Jenna heard about our lunch already.

"Don't worry. I walked into the Gulch for a cup of coffee"—she gestured with the cup she held in her hands—"and they asked me if our family had any news to announce. So give. What happened?"

I groaned. "Nothing. We drank a milkshake."

"And?" Jenna wouldn't let go.

"Do you mind if we don't tell the world my private business?" I twisted the doorknob and walked inside.

Jenna followed me. "I'm waiting."

"Audie held my hand. No big deal."

"Aha! My little sister has finally plunged into the rivers of love." She hugged me and danced in the direction of the hats on display along my front counter. "You better be careful. Before long they'll be accusing you of two-timing Cord."

"There's nothing between Cord and me. There has never been anything serious." Why did my heart protest as I said the words?

"I know that. You always followed the six-inch rule

on your dates. But you know that townspeople have linked your names ever since you were born a month apart. Don't you worry about that." She twirled around and took my hands in hers, her hazel eyes searching my face. "But I suspect that Audie is a different matter. If I lived here, I might want him for myself."

I blushed, thinking of the kiss we shared only last night.

Of course Jenna noticed. "I'm right! It's about time you found someone for yourself." She picked up a cloche and tried it on.

"Not that one." I was glad for an excuse to get Jenna's attention off of my romantic life. "I have just the hat for you." I opened a hatbox and proudly displayed an original Hattie Carnegie creation. "As soon as I saw this, I thought of you." Made from black velvet, tiny white beads dotted the top like stars, while a starburst eye blinked in the center.

Jenna gasped and put it on her head at an angle. She looked in the cosmetics mirror I kept on top of the glass case. "I'm Lucy!"

I smiled. Trust Jenna to know that Lucille Ball favored Hattie Carnegie creations. "Use these." I handed her a couple of beaded hat pins. The flashy beads shone like rubies against her hair.

What a difference a hat can make. A simple black hat transformed my sister from a twenty-first century standout to a 1940s-era vamp. Jenna turned her head and looked at herself from every angle.

"I'll take it, of course." Jenna dug in her purse for her credit card. I might give a bonnet to Enid

Waldberg, but Jenna could afford to pay. She ordered from my store via the Internet from time to time. If I gave her everything she fancied, I'd go broke.

"I'll give you the usual ten percent discount." I rang up the purchase. "Do you want me to wrap it up for you?"

"No, thanks. I'll wear it out the door." Jenna signed the receipt. "I came in to say good-bye. I've already missed a day of work, and I'm on deadline." Jenna had parlayed an interest in video games as a teenager into a lucrative career creating computer games. Since she moved to Taos, she also started dealing in contemporary western art. Successful in business if not in love, she had always paid her own way, and Dina's, too. Dina could go to any college she wanted.

"What about Dina?" I said. I couldn't believe my sister would abandon her daughter as long as she was still a suspect in a murder investigation.

Jenna tossed her head, her sleek blond hair falling back into perfect place, the new hat clinging to her skull. "She doesn't need me. She's got you and Dad and Cord and now Audie. For that matter, she's probably got the whole community of Grace Gulch behind her. She doesn't need me. She never has."

That's where you're wrong. An entire community couldn't take a mother's place. But I didn't say the words. Jenna wouldn't believe it now, any more than she had any time in the past nineteen years.

Grabbing the bag with the hatbox and receipt, Jenna marched to the door. "Just be sure nothing happens to my baby." With those parting words, she left us behind, like she always did.

Jenna's flight from responsibility shouldn't surprise me, but my frustration demanded release. I wanted to tear up something. Anything. I posted a sign that read RING BELL FOR SERVICE and headed for the back room.

Tomorrow was trash pickup day. Usually I sorted through boxes and paper, recycling what I could and discarding the rest. Not today.

A stack of empty boxes in the back left corner seemed like a good place to start. Some items arrived in hand-packed boxes, wrapped with simple paint tape.

"That no-good sister of mine." I flattened one box, slamming down the sides with my fist. "Will she ever take care of anyone besides herself?" I started on a second box. "Or will she always leave me holding the baby?" No one ever asked what I wanted. My family needed me. So I stayed in Grace Gulch. I might have stayed anyhow, but I wanted a say in the matter. But Jenna had made the choices for all of us.

Before long the pile of boxes lay flat on a pallet. I had given Jenna's behavior over to God long ago, but this weekend had stirred up old resentments. I simply couldn't believe that she would let Dina face possible murder charges alone.

By the time I finished, soft tissue paper was strewn on the floor, useless now that I had tramped it underfoot. Stupid of me. Now I would need to replace it, an unnecessary expense.

The bell rang. A customer! I took a deep breath and walked at a deliberate pace into the store.

I searched my memory to place the face. Stacy

Ward, a cousin of some kind to Mitch Gaynor. She belonged to the Gulch's scattered family; if I remembered correctly, nowadays she lived somewhere in Kansas. "How may I help you?"

"I saw all those beautiful costumes at the concert on Sunday," Stacy said. "Someone mentioned that you had provided most of them. I thought you might be able to suggest something for me."

If the short, stout lady hoped one of my costumes would restore her Gibson-girl figure, she was doomed to disappointment. But I excelled at matching style to customer. "Dresses from the Gay Nineties and the early 1900s are over here." I directed her to the depleted rack of period costumes. We found a suit in light blue silk that didn't throw her body into an *S* curve but rather made the most of her coloring. Another customer came in while I was ringing up the sale. My cell phone rang, but I couldn't answer it. By the time they left, my emotions had cooled down.

Audie had left a message. "I'll be there at five thirty. Plan on dinner."

Audie. The sound of his voice sent my emotions flying again. What had Jenna said—something about wanting him for herself?

I whipped the empty hangers from the dress rack with more force than necessary. Did it really matter that much? I retrieved a few more dresses and hung them on the Centennial rack. More people came in.

They poked around the store. "Do you have anything on sale?"

"I might have a sale next week. For the best

selection, you should shop now."

As I expected, they browsed through the store and left without buying. I urged a catalog on both of them—"in case you change your mind."

Jenna had breezed in and out of our lives again like those shoppers, looking for the best bargain.

Jenna had her career. She had New Mexico. She had freedom. She had—the world!

She couldn't have Audie, too.

9

September 18, 1891 Excerpt A
Dearest Mary,
It is finally happening! A second chance! The
Cherokee Commission has completed negotiations for
purchasing land from the Iowa, Sac, Fox, Pottawatomie,
and Shawnee, and the date for the next land run has
been set for four days hence, Tuesday, September 22nd.

My dreams are flying as high as the red-tailed hawk
that I watch soaring overhead in a sky as clear as the
water in our river. We will have our ranch. I am sure
of it. God would not have brought us this far to fail us
now.

Monday, September 23

When I thought about it, I realized of course that
Jenna didn't want Audie. But she sometimes understood
me better than I understood myself. She had seen
through my protests to my heart, and she wanted to
open my eyes to my true feelings—in her own unique
way, of course. I cared about Audie. A lot.

Maybe I was giving too much credit to my sister, or maybe I had guessed the truth. How could I look Audie in the eye tonight? Would he want to hold my hand? Kiss me—again? Suddenly I wished I had chosen to wear something a little more feminine than my walking suit.

Don't be silly. I dressed to please myself, and the outfit was both comfortable and practical in light of my workday. I rearranged the hats on the front counter into a pleasing line and studied the rest of the store layout. With the Land Run festivities over, the store could use a front window display from a different era. I had fun featuring different times in Oklahoma history, gathering photographs of famous Oklahomans, brief bios, and descriptions of their outfits, with clothing and accessories for sale.

Kate Barnard, who moved to Oklahoma in the 1890s and became the first woman elected to a state office in 1907, graced my Land Run Days window. I liked selling a bit of history with my merchandise. I kept a few books on fashion for sale; Dina teased me about that, saying that I was running a clothing store, not a library. I didn't see it that way. Cici's Vintage Clothing opened a door into the past, and the books added detail.

Before I could decide on what to feature next, business picked up. Customers came in, two or three at a time. Several stopped to look at the books; some of the shyer types found more satisfaction in reading about history than in dressing the part. They bought enough of the books to make it worth the investment.

The front doorbell rang several times in the next hour. At four o'clock, I looked up in time to catch a glimpse of hair the color of spun gold entering the store—Suzanne Jay. Her appearance reminded me of my list of suspects. *Investigating will be easy if all of them seek me out.*

I waved a welcome and rang up the current customers. A mother and daughter had chosen a pillbox hat, an A-line dress for the mother, and a poodle skirt for the daughter. "Thank you for your business." I smiled. "Come again."

Suzanne made a beeline for the register. The red-spangled dress she had worn to dance the cancan at the concert was draped over her left arm. Her beautiful, bottle-blond hair had lost the bouffant bees' nest that made her stand out over the weekend. If anything, it looked deflated, sticking to her head as if she had combed out the teasing without bothering to wash it in between. Dark smudges marred the taut skin under her hazel eyes. The weekend must have worn her out.

The weekend. Now that I had the suspect in my sights, what should I ask her? I couldn't blurt out, *Did you kill Penn Hardy?*

Suzanne spread the garment across the counter. "I'm afraid I tore the dress when I was dancing yesterday."

"I can imagine. I've torn the hems in my own dresses with my heels."

"Your dress wasn't made for dancing." A small smile sprang to her lips then quickly disappeared "I watched you and your sisters from the wings. People loved it. I saw a few camera flashes."

I groaned. "Another chapter in the saga of the Wilde

sisters." Her words struck a chord. "Camera flashes, you say?" Mitch Gaynor sat in the front row, ready to record the highlights of the concert. He wouldn't! But he would. Anything to sell a paper, and he might choose to feature us instead of the clowns. I grabbed the morning's edition of the *Sequoian*, unread except for the front page. In small print, under the description of the concert, I read aloud, "For more pictures, see page 4." I ruffled the pages and found what I feared: a close-up and personal photograph of three pairs of kicking legs, our faces out of focus but recognizable. "The joys of living in a small town," I muttered.

"When do you think you can have my dress ready? I'm supposed to return it to Dina as soon as possible." As props person, Dina handled the dresses that I loaned to the theater group for the Land Run Days celebration.

Suzanne's words brought me back to the moment, and I set aside the embarrassing picture. I needed to weave the gunfight into the conversation before we finished business.

"Let me see." I found the rip and wondered how well I could hide a repair of the fragile silk. "The Gulch seemed to do brisk business during the festival. You certainly looked the part of a saloon proprietor in this dress." I marked another spot that needed to be cleaned. "I hardly saw you all weekend. You must have stayed busy. Did you get to see any of the play?"

"I wouldn't have missed it." Some of Suzanne's old verve was back, as if she had arrived on stage, ready to give a performance. "I made one of my helpers stay behind the bar when the crowd assembled outside."

She pointed a finger at me. "I saw you. You looked lovely in that beige dress."

I fought the blush that threatened to rise in my cheeks. I couldn't let her change the subject. "I can't believe what happened. Poor Penn. I didn't think he had an enemy in the world."

A bleak look clouded Suzanne's eyes, and she dropped her gaze. Her reaction seemed out of proportion to a casual acquaintance, or maybe I was overly suspicious. The front doorbell rang, and Audie walked in. "I decided to come early."

"You weren't supposed to learn about my little accident." Light had returned to Suzanne's eyes. "The dress has a tiny rip."

More like the Grand Canyon, I thought. But I had seen, and repaired, worse.

"And I've asked Cici to fix it for me."

The doorbell rang again. This time a couple of ladies that I didn't recognize entered the store. They headed straight for the front counter and studied the hat display.

The opportunity to question Suzanne further had passed. Maybe I could talk with her when she picked up her dress, although I didn't want to put it off that long.

"When will you have my dress ready?" The voice that could carry across a theater dropped below a whisper. Her attention seemed to be directed somewhere else, at the newcomers in the store.

"Wednesday morning," I said, and Suzanne turned to leave.

One of the customers tried on a cloche after she

signed the guest register and cocked her head to inspect the effect in the mirror. She seemed to notice us for the first time. The smile on her face faded.

"Mrs. Hardy," she said. "I didn't expect to see you here. I'm so sorry for your loss."

The words were directed at Suzanne.

Suzanne's face paled, and she sagged against the register. Audie sprang into action. He escorted her to a chair and brought her a glass of water while I assisted the customers. *Mrs. Hardy?* It didn't take Sherlock Holmes to deduce what that implied.

"I didn't realize you knew—Suzanne," I said. I glanced in her direction. She sat, cowed in the corner chair like a puppy being scolded after an accident.

"I work as a night clerk at a hotel down in Oklahoma City," the stranger said. "I remember her and her husband when they came for the weekend. They spent the night in our honeymoon suite. So sad for him to die that way, during the gunfight. Perhaps I shouldn't have said anything?"

"She knows you meant well." My mind was still trying to wrap itself around the idea of Suzanne and Penn together. "When was this? I, uh, didn't know they had taken a second honeymoon."

"About a month ago," she said.

I couldn't think what else to ask without sounding like a busybody. *Did they come more than once? Did you notice that Suzanne didn't wear a wedding ring? Where was Gwen while this was going on?*

We completed our business.

"Please convey our sympathy to Mrs. Hardy," the

customer said. She glanced to the corner where Audie knelt beside a sobbing Suzanne. I promised and turned the sign on my door to CLOSED after she departed.

"You must think I'm horrible," Suzanne said.

"These past few days must have been difficult for you," Audie said. "I must say you put on a good face. If you want to talk about it, we're ready to listen."

Good thinking. Here was a perfect opportunity to get Suzanne to open up to us.

Audie's kind words stemmed the flow of Suzanne's tears a little. "You don't know how miserable it's been. I've wanted to hole up and cry, but I've had to carry on and pretend like nothing happened." Suzanne sniffled and raised her head in a theatrical gesture. "I'm an actress, after all."

"How long have, I mean, had you. . .known. . . Penn?"

"In the biblical sense, you mean?" Suzanne hiccuped a hysterical giggle. "We met when he was covering the opening of the MGM last spring. We liked each other and, well, one thing led to another." She dabbed at her face, her tears creating mud from the mascara and deepening the bags under her eyes.

"I'll get a washcloth." Audie disappeared in the direction of the bathroom.

"That weekend in Oklahoma City was our first time together. Very romantic. Every girl wants to be swept off her feet."

Not usually with another woman's husband. I refrained from saying so. I didn't want to stop the flow of Suzanne's chatter.

"He said all the usual things, I suppose. How

Gwen didn't really understand him and they only stayed together because of the kids, but they were older now, and he and I could start a new life together." She must have sensed my skepticism. "Oh, I know, it all sounds so trite when I say it out loud, but I believed him. I wanted to believe him."

I tried to remember what Audie had told me of Suzanne's past. At least one failed marriage? Biological clock ticking and facing approaching middle age alone? A small amount of sympathy stirred in my heart.

Audie returned with a washcloth. Suzanne blinked tear-laden eyelashes at him. "Thank you, Audie. You're so kind." She offered a small smile.

"I'm surprised you managed to keep it a secret." I wanted her attention back on Penn. Why hadn't the gossip mill reported this juicy tidbit?

"Not completely, although we were very discreet. The police know about the. . .affair. They've already questioned me." She sniffed and looked at Audie in mute appeal. "I wonder if Gwen mentioned me to them. Penn said she was getting suspicious."

I thought about the name and address of the customer who had just left and wondered if I should give the information to Chief Reiner.

Audie asked the question that was on my mind.

"What did the police say?"

"They consider me a 'person of interest.'" Suzanne said the words like a character in a police drama. "They asked me where I was during the gunfight. I told them that I was on the sidewalk, along with half the population of Lincoln County."

Suzanne looked as though she was going to cry again. She dabbed at her face with the damp washcloth. I dragged a chair from behind the register and sat down next to her, trying to model my expression after Enid Waldberg, someone with a compassionate and listening ear. There had to be more to her story.

"Then they asked if I had handled the gun Cord used during the gunfight. During rehearsals, they said. I told that detective. . .you know, the guy with the Teddy Roosevelt mustache and the paunch that hangs over his belt?"

"Chief Reiner?"

"I told him that I hadn't been at the rehearsals for the gunfight because I wasn't in the play. But yes, I had seen the gun. Cord liked showing it off. Apparently it's a collector's item. I told Reiner that I could hardly tell a rifle from a revolver and I didn't pay much attention." She sniffed. "They said they would be talking with Cord. I suppose he's a 'person of interest,' as well."

Audie and I looked at each other. We knew about the confrontation between Cord and the chief outside the MGM the afternoon of the concert.

"Penn was going to leave his wife for you. . ." I let the words trail off.

"He was getting cold feet." Suzanne's voice carried like a stage whisper. "I think he had changed his mind." Tears overflowed. "Oh, Audie, you have to help me! They think I killed Penn when I discovered that he would never leave Gwen for me!" She clutched his arm and dragged him down to his knees beside her, heedless of the tears drenching his sleeve.

What a character, I thought. Suzanne's lover wasn't even underground yet, and she had already pegged Audie as her new savior.

"Of course we'll help you, any way we can." Audie spoke in the same calm voice he used to defuse tensions on the stage. Why was he promising to help her? Didn't he remember that she was on our list of suspects? Jealousy flared up in me, red and hot.

Audie extricated himself from Suzanne's grasp and took the washcloth. "Here. Let me freshen this for you." While he went to the restroom, I uncovered the box of tissues I kept behind the register and handed it to Suzanne. She didn't speak again until Audie returned.

"Who was standing near you when Penn was shot?" Audie asked. "Maybe one of them had a reason to kill him."

"The mayor was there. Gwen. I remember her, because we bumped into each other and made polite excuses, like two boxers meeting in the center ring. Dina, but you know that." Suzanne mentioned a few other visitors; she had chatted with them at the bar and remembered their names. If she ever gave up acting, she could have a terrific career as a waitress. She did it well. She mentioned everyone on our list and a few more. "That other newspaper man was there, too. Mitch Gaynor."

"Do you know if any of them have a reason for hating Penn?" Audie asked. "Did Penn mention anything about any of them when you were together?"

"Not really. All he ever talked about was work. And his family." Anger cut into the sorrow on Suzanne's face.

"At first I didn't mind. I figured he needed a shoulder to cry on, about how badly Gwen was treating him. But it got old pretty quick. He carried on and on about how he needed more money for some business deal."

This was news. How did he plan to raise money? "Did he give you any particulars?"

"No." Suzanne shook her head. "I got the impression he was working on some kind of deal at the paper."

"Did he talk about people he worked with?" I admit, I was curious to see if she would mention Dina. "Any stories? Any nasty letters to the editor?" We could look through the *Herald* archives for some of this information, but Penn might have mentioned something off the record to Suzanne.

"Not recently. Work became an excuse not to see me. We'd plan to meet, and he would call and say he had to work late." Anger twisted her features. "I was a distant third in his life. First there were his kids and then his work. He saw me when he could fit me in. I might have ended things myself unless something changed." She stared at us, as if aware of how that sounded. "I would have stopped seeing him. I don't mean that I would *kill* him."

"Of course not," Audie murmured.

I could have throttled him for his easy agreement. I wouldn't let her off so easily.

"You said you thought Gwen suspected something was going on. Do you think she might want to kill him?"

"I don't know." Suzanne shrugged helplessly. "Penn

said all the fire had gone out of their marriage a long time ago, but you never know."

"The kids?" Audie asked. "Teens often carry a grudge against their parents."

I tried to remember if the Hardy children appeared on our sketch. I didn't think so.

"Hah." Suzanne snorted. "Daughter dearest couldn't wait to leave home. At least that's the impression I had. Penn had a decent relationship with her, I guess, but she was ready to try her wings. He didn't talk about his son much." She wiped her face clean of tears and makeup with a tissue, revealing a pale, tired women. "What excited him the most was work. You could count on him getting fired up about some story or other." Suzanne smiled at the memory. "Like a hound on the scent of a fox, you know? Baying furiously and running as hard as he could to chase the story down. He was a good newspaperman."

"What was he working on most recently?" I asked.

"Something big." She brightened. "Penn said it could be the biggest thing of his career."

"And?" Audie asked.

"And nothing. He didn't tell me any details." Suzanne looked at the two of us. "You will help me, won't you? Help me figure out the real murderer?" A few tears dripped from the ends of her eyelashes. "Penn wasn't the best of men, but he didn't deserve to die."

September 18, 1891 Excerpt B

*Now that the date is set, I am ready to lay aside
the weights which beset me, as God advises us to do in
Hebrews. Ethan has offered to purchase my few possessions
for a fair price. He will also hold any items that I wish to
retain so that Patches may run the race light and swift. All
I will carry is my canteen, bedroll, and rifle.*

*I have seen Mr. Gaynor in town making
preparations. I fear he plans to run for the same land.
The gulch is divided into more than one plot, but I want
the best for us.*

—

Monday, September 23

A cup of hot tea, a couple of frosted sugar cookies,
and thirty minutes later, I closed the door behind
Suzanne with a little more force than necessary. I
sagged against the doorframe, surprise and tension
draining me of energy.

"What a shocker." I grimaced. The sky started its
daily dance with sunset, pink and lavender drifting
with the clouds. "Do you think it's too late in the day

to pay a condolence call?"

"I don't know." Audie shrugged. "Maybe Gwen will open up to us more if she's hungry and not thinking straight."

I grimaced. "Or she may hurry us away so she can eat her supper."

I took the cash drawer out of the register and frowned when I discovered a bill laid in the wrong direction, face side up. "What about Suzanne?" I asked, counting the bills as I cashed out the drawer. "She seems like a good suspect to me. We already knew she had opportunity and now we know she had a whopper of a motive."

"That doesn't mean that she did it. We need to talk with everyone on our list. Can I help you close up?"

I showed him where to store the more pricy items, in a locked closet at the back of the storage room. Jewelry went in the wall safe with cash.

"Why couldn't it be Suzanne?" I swept cookie crumbs from the floor and threw them in the trash can.

"I haven't ruled Suzanne out. It's just my impression. She was heartbroken."

Silly man. Taken in by a sob story. "Heartbroken, maybe, but why? By Penn's death...or because he dumped her?"

"You sound like she's already been tried and found guilty." Audie pulled down the blinds against the westward facing windows. "I'm only saying that there are two sides to every story and we need to find out what Gwen has to say before we rush to judgment."

"You're right." I made one more turn around the

store. "Okay, I'm ready to go." I wrapped the remaining cookies in a napkin. "Here's a peace offering. Who knows, maybe they'll do more good than another casserole. Dina and I are supposed to take her supper later this week."

Audie shrugged. "I don't have much experience with small-town funeral etiquette. With funerals of any kind, really. Thank God."

"Enid is organizing a week of meals from the church." I locked the front door, and we exited from the back. "We like to take care of each other around here."

"You're ready to give Gwen the benefit of the doubt but not Suzanne?" Audie sounded amused.

"At least they were married." I felt ashamed of myself. When had I become such a Pharisee in my attitudes?

"I think it's great that the church helps out in times like this. Love in action."

After Audie said that, I felt better. And guilty. I'd focused on the suspicions surrounding Dina and Cord to the exclusion of the grief Penn's widow must feel. *If she's innocent*, a persistent voice in my mind repeated.

Enid was pulling out of Gwen's driveway as we drove up. She motioned for us to stop and rolled down her window. "I'm so glad you decided to come by. I just delivered supper to Gwen," she said. "I hope she will invite you to stay for the meal. She asked me, but I had a previous commitment with Paul. If you do, maybe she'll eat. She's not looking well."

I remembered how I hadn't wanted to eat for weeks

after my mother died.

"Of course we will," Audie said. "Cici?"

I nodded my agreement. "And we'll stay to clean up after the meal. Don't worry."

On our way to the front door, we passed a windsock decorated with a white bull against a navy blue background, the logo of the Grace Gulch Bulls. Gwen Hardy waited behind the glass, her normally thin face turned into an El Greco painting by grief. She opened the door and waved us in. "Cici. Audie. How good of you to stop by."

The three of us stood in the front hallway for a minute, waiting for someone to speak.

"We're so sorry about Penn." Audie spoke in a low voice, his hands tucked in the back pockets of his jeans as if he didn't know what to do with them.

It's up to me. I sniffed the air. "Something sure smells good. Are we interrupting your supper?"

"Enid brought over a lovely meal. You just missed her. The Word of Truth family has been wonderful. They've promised to bring food every day this week."

"We ran into her on the street. Here's my contribution." I thrust the wrapped cookies at her. "I'm supposed to bring a meal later this week, but I brought this tonight."

"Would you care to join us?" Gwen at last offered the invitation. "We have enough to feed an army."

"We'd love to." *I thought you'd never ask.*

The meal passed mostly in silence. Both Audie and I made appreciative noises over the fare—country cooking at its finest—chicken and dumplings with bacon-flavored green beans and fresh peach cobbler. The boy, Sammy, ate a few bites and then excused himself and disappeared into the study. Soon we heard the rat-a-tat of video game gunfire. Grief takes different forms, I guess. I stopped myself from taking a second helping of cobbler. The more nervous I am, the more I tend to eat. Instead, I busied myself with clearing the table. Audie joined me, multiple dishes stacked in his arms.

"Whoa! Be careful!"

"Don't worry. I didn't break a single dish during my starving actor days, when I waited on tables for my day job." He gracefully stacked them by the sink. "Why don't you make some fresh coffee? Decaf, if she has any."

I dutifully searched the cupboards, although the likelihood of finding decaf in any red-blooded Oklahoman's home was about as likely as a snowstorm in the Sahara. My love of caramel truffle decaf made me the exception to the rule. "How about some herbal tea?" I grabbed a tray from the top shelf while Audie stacked the dishwasher. It felt natural to work as a team. He seemed right at home. I imagined him in my kitchen, swirling a pasta sauce while I tossed a salad. I smiled to myself, pleased at the image. I bet he liked something more adventurous than chicken-fried steak in his diet, although he had taken to Oklahoma cooking with pleasure.

"Are we ready?" He held the mirrored tray I had fixed with mugs of passion plum tea, the sugar cookies I had brought, and iris-flowered napkins.

Gwen had returned to the front room. The straight-backed chair she sat in looked like it was the only thing keeping her upright. However, the meal had brought some color to her face. A hint of life returned, and she smiled at the sight of Audie with the tray.

"Thank you so much. My favorite tea and sugar cookies. I bet you got them from Gaynor Goodies." Tears sprang to her eyes. "The kids gave us that tray for our last wedding anniversary." She used one of the napkins to dab at her eyes. "Everywhere I look, something reminds me of Penn."

"Hold on to those happy thoughts." The words came from someplace deep inside me, emotions remembered from the days following my mother's death. "That's the way he lives on."

"Happy thoughts." Gwen laughed a little, in a way that suggested there were a number of unhappy ones, as well. "One of the things Penn really enjoyed was the theater. He was so pleased when Mrs. Mallory hired you, Audie. He fancies—fancied—himself as some kind of amateur actor." She smiled at some memory.

"I think we're all actors at heart. Oscar Wilde said, 'I regard the theater as the greatest of all art forms, the most immediate way in which a human being can share with another the sense of what it is to be a human being.' We were glad to have Penn in the play. We approached Mitch Gaynor about playing his grandfather's part, but he refused. Suzanne Jay suggested Penn, and he jumped at the chance. I didn't know he was a Gaynor until then."

On his mother's side. I filled in the blank mentally.

Gwen paused in mid-bite and set her cookie back on the napkin. "Oh, yes, Miss Jay. She played the part of a saloon girl so perfectly, almost as if she had rehearsed the role in real life." She took another small bite and chewed. Listening to her, I knew we had our answer. She had known about Penn's affair with Suzanne, and it had mattered to her. It still did. A lot.

"I'm glad to hear you shared a lot of happy memories with Penn." I decided to strike. "You hear about so many unhappy marriages these days."

Gwen stirred a spoonful of sugar into her mug and took a sip. A myriad of emotions played across her face. I wondered what she would decide to share, if anything.

"Our marriage wasn't perfect. No marriage is." She ran her finger around the edge of the tray, tracing the delicate pattern. "But it was built to last. I meant it when I said, 'Till death do us part.'" Her face crumpled. "And now death has parted us, long before it was meant to happen. I've lost him forever." A few tears fell, but she regained her composure.

Interesting that she used first person singular to describe her wedding vows. Was the commitment to the marriage one-sided? Of course we knew about Penn's infidelity, but had he taken steps to get out of his marriage? Did Gwen want Penn so badly that if she couldn't have him, no one could—even if it meant murder?

Audie caught my eye and made a circle with his index finger. I recognized the gesture from rehearsals. Wrap it up.

"Mrs. Hardy—" he began.

"Gwen, please."

"Gwen. May I ask you about the play?"

Gwen turned her hands over in a resigned gesture. "Certainly."

Audie paused, as if considering his words, before continuing. "Penn was so excited about writing the play for the reenactment." Audie wrapped his long fingers around a slate blue mug. "I think it was the best of both worlds for him. The research intrigued his journalistic instincts, and writing the play allowed him to indulge the artist. He certainly had a way with words."

Gwen settled back in her chair, a wistful look temporarily transforming her into the young beauty who had captured Penn's heart. "He used to write poetry for me. Most of it was pretty awful. He thought it was cute that our names rhymed—Gwen and Penn, you know—and he used every possible rhyme he could think of and even made up a few words. I was carried away by the romance of it all." Her lips relaxed, soft, comfortable. "No one had ever written poetry for me before."

I tried to imagine a young Penn Hardy so smitten that he wrote sappy love poems. What had happened along the way to make him turn to Suzanne? Had Gwen's feelings changed as well—from poetic enchantment to darker tales of murder? I looked at our hostess and doubted it. The grief in her face had softened with the happy memories, but her clothes still spoke volumes of grief. Not the unrelieved black of the Victorian era, but a more modern version. Her careless combination of a polka dot blouse with plaid slacks said a lot about overwhelming feelings that allowed her to commit a fashion faux pas.

And how did we get so far from the subject of the play? I wondered what point Audie was trying to uncover. Where did he want to steer the conversation?

"He did some of that with the play. Told some of the story in rhyme. 'Did Grace try to save a space, seeking to win the race/or did he win fair and square, beating out his foe Gay-nair.' " His deadpan mimic made Penn come to life in the room.

"Yes." Gwen choked on her laughter. "The Ballad of Grace Gulch. He wanted to publish it in the *Herald*. I warned him to be careful of a libel suit. Bob Grace's ghost would haunt him to the grave even if all he wanted to do was poke fun at the old feud."

"Do you think he had the facts of the story straight?" Audie leaned forward in his chair. "I was a little surprised when the play repeated the traditional story of the land run. I heard he had found some of Bob Grace's old letters."

"Those letters!" Momentary fury twisted Gwen's face. She pulled a burlap sack with crackling paper sounds from under a side table. "I wish he had never found the stupid things."

"Where did he run across them?"

"Oh, when he was rummaging through old papers at the office, looking for information about the land run. Why didn't he leave well enough alone? If he had never decided to tell the true story of Grace Gulch—as he put it—and if he'd never taken part in your play, maybe he'd still be alive."

She shoved the sack of Audie. "Take them. I don't ever want to see them again." Tears gathered in her nutmeg-brown eyes, ready to overflow in a cascade of love lost. "Please leave." We had to lean forward to catch her words. "I'd like to be alone."

We said farewell and departed, leaving Gwen alone in the darkened living room, with only the mirrored tray to remind her of happier times.

"I feel awful," I told Audie. "She seemed in better spirits when we arrived than when we left."

"Maybe she just needs to cry." Audie spoke as if he had been comforting grieving widows all his life. "We're trying to help. If we can bring Penn's murderer to justice, that should bring her some comfort."

That won't help her sleep tonight. I looked out the window at the side of the road. Last night's rain had loosened dirt and scattered it in red rivulets across the pavement. It shone a rusty red, like dried blood, in the artificial light. I shuddered. "Both Gwen and Suzanne seem genuinely upset by Penn's death. They responded so differently, though."

"You could say they stayed in character," Audie said, turning on the heater. The night air had grown a little chilly. "Suzanne did, at least. I don't know Gwen all that well."

"That's true. Suzanne was as dramatic as usual, whereas Gwen has always been kind of quiet. Her outburst there at the end surprised me."

"It sounds like there might be dynamite in those papers. I can't wait to take a look at them." He glanced at me. "We've talked with two of the suspects. Your impressions?"

A car whizzed past us, blaring its horn.

"Keep your eyes on the road." The reprimand

was unnecessary, and I regretted it as soon as the words came out. Audie drove carefully, and the fool that passed us came around the corner too fast. But I needed a moment to gather my thoughts. I wanted to believe in Suzanne's guilt, maybe because of the way she fawned over Audie and flirted with him before her lover was in the ground. But every motive that applied to her applied equally to Gwen.

"I wonder how long the affair had been going on. That clerk said she saw them last summer. Maybe three, four months?"

"That sounds logical. It started after I came to town. At least that's what Suzanne said. Here's a question: Did Gwen know about it?"

"Absolutely! You heard the way she reacted when you brought up Suzanne's name."

"Why, darlin', that was just a tribute to Suzanne's fine acting skills." Audie tried a bit of a John Wayne drawl. "I agree. She knew about it," he continued in his normal voice. "Next question. Was Suzanne his first?"

That stumped me. The citizens of Grace Gulch usually knew everyone else's business. But I hadn't heard about Suzanne. "I don't know. I don't think he could keep a string of infidelities quiet. He seemed to be a nice enough man, focused on work and family, just like Suzanne said. The kind that keeps a photo of his wife and kids on his desk. He came into my store to buy Gwen a special present for their last anniversary." Penn had chosen a peignoir set from 1982, the year they had wed.

"When was that?"

I searched my memory. "Last January, I think. After Christmas." I thought about the timing. "So it was before he took up with Suzanne."

Audie nodded. "It's a classic love story. Boy meets girl, or in this case, girl meets boy. Girl loses boy. That's where the twist comes in. Did one of them decide that murder was a better option than the third act, when girl gets the boy back? In that case, Gwen's our gal."

"But what about Suzanne?" I said. "What if she believed Penn's pack of lies about leaving his wife? Then she discovered that he was stringing her along?"

"Suzanne didn't murder him. Why are you focusing on her?" Annoyance laced Audie's words. "It's not like this was her first disappointment in love. She made some minor headlines when she tried her wings in Hollywood. She came to Oklahoma to escape all that, only, poor thing, she fell right back into the same trap."

Poor thing, my foot. *He sure has a blind spot for such a smart man.* Or was I the one with the blind spot? Jealousy bubbled up within me, hot and fierce. What an ugly emotion. *Lord, help me to seek the truth. Not what I want to see.*

"What do you think about Gwen, then?"

Audie shrugged his shoulders, a shadowy movement in the dark car. "Maybe. Still waters run deep and all that. I think she was angry enough. But I'm not convinced either one of them did it."

"Me neither." I pulled out Audie's sketch of the area in front of the saloon and peered at it under a passing streetlight. "Can you turn on the overhead light?"

Audie curbed the car and switched on the light. "What is it?"

I studied the placement of the figures. From where Suzanne was standing, it would take an expert marksman to make the shot.

Something, I was sure, she was not.

September 18, 1891 Excerpt C

Gaynor has a good stallion, a black beauty, sixteen hands tall, who looks as if he could win any race he entered. I wonder about Patches. I remember the last run and how other horses outran us.

I have lightened the load that he must carry in hopes of increasing his speed. The ride will be long and hard, over several hills and through thick woods. His experience and endurance should serve us well.

Nevertheless, I looked over animals on sale for the land run. I see more claims of "made the '89 run!" than are credible. Most of them are old nags, not strong enough for the journey.

I will stay with Patches and hope for the best.

Your loving fiancé,

Robert Grace

Monday, September 23

Back in Audie's Focus, I stared into the now-turquoise night. A hint of sunset lingered through a gap in the hills to the west, a thin band of brilliant-hued clouds. A hundred years ago, my great-grandfather might have looked upon the same sight. Didn't King Solomon say there is nothing new under the sun? I wondered if and how my ancestors dealt with murder and mayhem or if they accepted it as a normal part of pioneer life.

"It's still fairly early." Audie's voice interrupted my reverie. I glanced at the clock on the dashboard: five past eight. "Since we've already had dinner, I'd like to take a look at Grace's papers. How about you?"

"Sure. Do you really think they will hold a clue to Penn's murder?" They might.

"Maybe." Audie grinned. "I confess that I am nosy. I want to read Grace's side of the story about the infamous land run."

"Let's go to my house then." I had driven that day, in case I needed to shop or make deliveries.

Deliveries. I had intended to bring Suzanne's costume home tonight, make the needed repairs, and return it to her tomorrow. Oh, well. Audie's blind spot where she was concerned bothered me more than I cared to admit. Did he consider me too provincial— the Okie I was, in fact—in my attitude about Suzanne's affair with Penn? Maybe he imbibed the live-and-let-live philosophy of the theatrical community.

I couldn't. I knew as well as the next person that it only took one sin, any sin, to separate one from God, and that He extended His grace to everyone equally. But from a human perspective, the excesses common among the Hollywood crowd sickened me.

Families mattered. As frustrating as Dad, Dina, and

Jenna could be, they were always there, the foundation of my life. An adulterer might laugh family values in the face. I wondered about Audie's background. What roots did the man I had come to know over the past few months grow from? What about his father? I tried to imagine Audie in twenty-five years' time. Thin, fair hair would grow lighter as gray replaced the blond locks. Those piercing blue eyes diminished by spectacles, or maybe still shining thanks to laser surgery. Laughter lines on his forehead. He would age well.

"A penny for your thoughts," Audie said.

"Oh, I was thinking about. . .family history and stuff like that." I was glad the dark hid the blush coloring my cheeks. I didn't want to confess my image of him as an older man. "Tell me about your family."

"My parents are both living. They're still together, a blessing in this day and age."

"Any siblings?"

Audie shook his head. "But tons of cousins. Both of my parents came from large families."

An only child. Even worse than dealing with Jenna and Dina.

"It wasn't so bad. I used to make up plays to entertain myself," Audie said as if reading my mind. "I got to play all the parts."

We turned the corner to my house.

"Speaking of plays. I hope we discover the information Hardy used to write about the land run in Grace's papers." He sounded so cheerful, I suspected that he was mentally rubbing his hands together.

Audie pulled his Focus to the curb in front of my

house, cutting off further discussion. I walked straight in. Even after the murder last weekend, I hadn't bothered with locking my door. After all, the murderer hadn't come after me. Audie entered behind me and headed for the kitchen.

"Give me a minute to change into something from this century," I said. "Make yourself at home."

The sound of china rattling and water splashing followed me as I dashed upstairs. I wormed my way out of the walking dress I had worn for the day and looked for something more comfortable. Not my sweats. Audie had never seen me at my worst, and tonight was no time to start. Instead I chose a simple white blouse and navy blue slacks, with a pink cardigan for warmth. I let my hair out of the bun and pulled it back with a hair clip and added reading glasses I had purchased at the supermarket for a few dollars. I needed them for historic papers like the Grace documents with their faded and spidery handwriting, often cramped to fit the maximum number of words on a page.

By the time I made it downstairs, Audie had brewed a pot of tea—apple cinnamon, by the scent—and cut up one of the Granny Smiths that I kept in a basket on the table. He moved efficiently, apple peels and cores already disposed of, a new roll of paper towels hanging on a vertical towel rack. I hadn't expected my dreams of us working side by side in my kitchen to come true so soon.

A small avalanche of envelopes waited in the center of the table.

"Your gal Friday, reporting for duty." I grinned at him.

"Aye, aye, Dr. Watson. Come and join me." Audie looked at me and smiled in appreciation, as if I had dressed for a night at the opera. "I was trying to put the letters in chronological order, but it's slowgoing."

I picked up one of the envelopes. A shiver passed through me. I held living history in my hands. A bold black script addressed each envelope to a Miss Mary Langston in Abilene, Kansas. The postmarks, barely legible over the claret-colored two-cent stamps, ranged from Dodge City to various places in Texas. "The Chisholm Trail," I said.

"Wasn't Grace a cowboy before he settled down to ranch life?"

"I believe so."

"What about Gaynor?"

"Oh, he was a farmer. Another aspect of their feud—farmer vs. rancher."

We divided the pile between us. Pieces of paper as thin as parchment fell into my hands and opened the door to another way of life. I could almost breathe in the dust—well, that hadn't changed much, had it? And feel Grace's faithful pony Patches beneath me. These were the letters of a man deeply in love with his fiancée, a dreamer. Reading his tender expressions of love made me feel like a voyeur.

"I wish I could pick a posy of thistle and lace to bring to you. The day the land is mine, I will bring you flowers every day, if you like." Oh, to have someone love me like that. I looked again at the plate with apple slices, now reduced to two thin pieces. It was the kind of thoughtful thing that Bob Grace might have done for his Mary. His practical concerns about the dangers of childbirth and the harsh realities of pioneer life also touched me.

"He mentions Gaynor." Audie looked up from the letter he was reading. "He knew they were both going to make the run for the same piece of land. And it sounds like Gaynor had the better horse. Bigger, at any rate."

"So the feud started before the actual race. If there was a race, if Grace actually did make the run and wasn't a 'Sooner' who camped out on the land ahead of time, like Gaynor always claimed."

"I haven't seen anything about that yet."

We continued reading. Audie chuckled. "He describes the land as a 'piece of Eden.' I confess that's not what jumped to my mind when I decided to move to Oklahoma." He must have seen the hurt expression on my face, because he hastened to add, "But first impressions can be deceiving. I was expecting flat fields of waving grain, not trees as thick as a primeval forest on the way in and out of town. Or the constant rise and fall of the back roads."

"People don't always realize how diverse Oklahoma is. The high plains start in western Oklahoma. Texas, too. Eastern Oklahoma is very green." I started another letter. "It appears that Mary Grace did her part to make it a garden. Maybe she planted some of the pecan trees that thrive here."

"I did see a reference to peach and apple trees. Were there really so many people eager to make the run?"

"Usually about three times as many people showed

up as there were potential homesteads. I've often wondered what happened to the others. Some of them sold everything just to reach for their dreams."

"Grace writes about that."

We continued reading in silence without finding anything. I opened the last envelope, dated September 19, 1891. I blinked and read it again. *"I will do whatever I must to secure land for our future."*

"I've found it." My voice trembled. "It looks like Gaynor was right. Grace planned to be on the land before the run."

"What?" Audie's brows shot up.

I handed the thin sheet to Audie.

"'I am ready to cheat. . .I have found a cave where I can hide. . .'" He read the words out loud. "Gaynor was right all along." He sounded disappointed. "It's hard to believe Grace would put his plan on paper. Wasn't it illegal?"

I shrugged. "Why not? He was mailing the letter to someone who wouldn't receive it until after the deed was done. And he shared everything with Mary." My mind reeled with the implications. "But this is not the story Penn wrote for the reenactment. He used the traditional story, Grace's revisionist history. Why? Did he ever discuss it with you?"

Audie shook his head. "He said he had found some interesting information in the letters that he intended to use. I got the feeling that his journalistic interest was aroused, and I expected to see a complete report in last weekend's edition of the *Herald*. He had unearthed some photos from around the time of the land run.

But he didn't print the story."

Possibilities raced through my mind. Suzanne said Penn was working on a big story. In Grace Gulch, no story would interest people more than the possible overturn of our sacred history. Didn't she also say that he was working on some get-rich-quick scheme?

An ugly thought crossed my mind. No one took Grace Gulch's history more seriously than Mayor Ron. And his name, the one I had considered the least likely and the most laughable, appeared on our list of suspects.

"Tell me about the newspapers," Audie said. "I'm guessing that Grace and Gaynor each started a paper back in the day."

"Yes." My voice sounded hoarse to my ears. "Gaynor named his paper after the famous educator Sequoyah, the one who invented the Cherokee alphabet. Grace laughed at that, said that Grace Gulch lay on former Sac-Fox land, not Cherokee, and started up the *Herald*." I thinned my lips in a smile. "In anything short of a world war, they were very partisan. Now, if you are a Grace, you take your news to the *Herald*; but if you're a Gaynor, you go to the *Sequoian*."

"And if you're neither?"

"I put ads in both papers."

Audie laughed. "Even so, it was probably in Penn's best interests to stick to the traditional story of the land run. Anything else and Mayor Ron might run him out of town."

I didn't dare to voice my own suspicions. That's all I had to go on, really, a suspicion, a whiff of an idea, no more substantial than smoke. What if Penn showed the letters to the mayor in an effort to blackmail him? Mayor Ron would do anything to protect the Grace family name—but did that include murder?

"I like your mayor."

So did I. Mayor Ron had the support of everyone except the most rabid Gaynors.

"I couldn't believe his office, the first time I saw it. All that memorabilia from different cities named Grace. North Dakota, Idaho—"

"Even New Zealand. He jokes about retiring there." I hoped my suspicions were unfounded, but now that they had lodged in my mind, I felt compelled to investigate the possibility. Weariness washed over me, and I wanted to lay my head on the table. It had been a long day. I folded the offending letter and stuffed it back in the envelope.

Audie followed my example, refolding thin sheets of letter paper and tucking them inside envelopes. "There is one more thing I wanted to discuss with you."

"Let me make more tea." I didn't really want the beverage, but my tumultuous thoughts needed a chance to subside. What did he want to talk about? Persuade me to drop the investigation? Back out of helping me? Ask for Jenna's phone number? The kettle took a minute to reheat while I rinsed out our mugs. No more sugar for me tonight, I decided. I would take my orange spice tea black.

By the time I finished fixing the tea, Audie had tidied up the letters and moved them to the small escritoire that I kept in my kitchen.

He stirred in a teaspoon of sugar and took a sip. "I wanted to talk to you about Suzanne."

My heart plummeted. *He's interested in her. I knew it.*

"I've been praying for her. I pray for everyone involved with the theater. But I'll redouble my efforts now. I had no idea that she was so unhappy."

"Pray for her?" I echoed his words in a high-pitched squeal. "Oh, of course." Here I was feeling jealous, and Audie was getting all spiritual and high-minded on me.

"More than anything else, she needs Jesus."

Audie, the apostle to the theater crowd. He put me to shame. When I opened my business, I intended to share the faith of our fathers—perhaps I should say the faith of our mothers since we carried hardly any menswear—with my customers along with their clothing. And how seldom I succeeded.

"Of course you're right." I swallowed my tea in an effort to hide my embarrassment. "And Gwen, too, to get through this awful time."

"Absolutely. And I'll be praying for your sister. Jenna, I mean. Dina is already on my prayer list."

And me? We did work together on the theater. I thought of my own spotty prayer journal and felt ashamed once again.

"Jenna?" I said out loud. Maybe the spark I thought I had seen wasn't a figment of my imagination.

"She seems so. . .well, confused. Unsettled. You are a solid rock. You've put down deep roots here. She's a wandering soul."

"Is that a bad thing or a good thing?"

"It's a good thing, for you. You're an anchor. You, your faith, your good sense. Jenna needs you, you know."

Yeah, I knew that. Experts said the middle child usually played peacemaker in the family. How Jenna passed the eldest child's role of caretaker on to me flumoxed me. I sighed.

"You're an amazing person, Cici. You're the glue that holds your family together. You take care of your dad. You practically raised Dina by yourself. You're a successful businesswoman. And now you're showing another aspect of your character—a twenty-first-century Jane Marple, jumping into this investigation." His eyes crinkled in silent merriment. "A trailblazer, caretaker, independent spirit. You epitomize the pioneer spirit."

I blinked. I looked into Audie's eyes, as clear and deep as Lake Tenkiller, and saw nothing there but sincerity. He reached across the table and clasped my right hand between both of his. Something unspoken hung between us.

He shuffled to his feet without letting go of my hand. His lips brushed my cheek. "And someday soon, when this mess is behind us, we'll talk more." He released my hand, and the magic spell ended.

A few moments later, I heard the door close and a car engine start. I stayed at the table, staring into the cooling tea, while thoughts whirled through my head. A smile stretched my face so far that it hurt.

Audie liked all the things about me that made me feel like a country woman who would never amount to anything outside of Grace Gulch. And he had hinted at a much deeper emotion.

Bursting with joy, I jumped up from the table, rinsed out the mugs, and changed for bed. After the uproar of the day, I had expected a sleep-deprived night, the many revelations of the day repeating themselves endless times in my thoughts.

Instead, Audie's compliments replayed themselves in my memory. Buoyed by his good opinion, I fell into a deep sleep.

September 19, 1891 Excerpt A
Dearest Mary,
It is happening again. Just like in April of '89, people are gathering at the border of the unassigned lands by the thousands. So many people are hungry for a fresh start. Working their own land would be a dream come true. Already twice as many people have assembled as there is land available, and I expect the numbers to soar to twenty thousand or more.

Dearest, my hope for a better result in this run is fast disappearing. What shall we do if I fail?

So I place my faith in God and in my pony. And wonder if there is more I should do.

Tuesday, September 24

When I awoke the next morning, my first thought was of Audie's amazing confession, and my good mood persisted. I decided to wear one of my favorite ensembles—this time a post–World War II dress, a pink floral design that did nice things for my figure, with three-quarter-length sleeves and a V-neck trimmed with white lace, belted with a silver buckle, the luxuriant feel of real silk on my legs. As usual, my hair took the longest time to fix. Manipulating my bangs into a high curl over my forehead with a curling iron, I pulled back the rest into a French twist.

I stopped by Gaynor's Goodies for a bag of tea cakes and managed to leave without spilling everything I had learned to the town gossip. I arrived at the store in time to brew a pot of coffee before nine. Today's outfit had inspired me to plan a 1940s front window display. I had posters of Joan Crawford and Rita Hayworth, those two prototypical pinup girls. Creating a window around their fashions would be fun. As for an Oklahoman, I would look to Angie Debo, the "First Lady of Oklahoma History." Surfing the Internet for further ideas, I ran across a picture of a platinum blond Veronica Lake and remembered Suzanne.

I'm supposed to be investigating a murder. The window can wait. I poured myself a cup of coffee and sat behind the cash register with the day's newspapers. Both reported a lack of progress by the police in the death of Penn Hardy. The *Sequoian* held out for the tragic accident theory. The *Herald* pounded on the police for a more thorough investigation.

The phone rang, interrupting my thoughts. I picked up the receiver.

"Hey, Cici! Did you see the paper this morning?" Cord usually didn't get a chance to read the news until after he finished his morning chores. But Penn's death had the whole town seeking out information. "The editor seems to agree with us that it was murder."

"I noticed that. Speaking of the murder, listen to what we learned yesterday." I thought Cord would like to know the list of suspects.

"We? As in you and that city boy?"

Oh, boy. I should have made that first-person singular. "Yes, Audie helped me talk with some people." I told Cord about the suspects we had identified and what we had learned about Suzanne and Gwen.

Cord whistled. "The classic love triangle. It can create all kinds of bad feelings."

I had a feeling that he was talking about more than Gwen and Suzanne.

"Promise me you'll be careful, won't you?"

I couldn't promise that, and Cord knew it. We hung up, both of us unsettled after the conversation.

I decided to peruse the mini-morgue I kept of both the *Herald* and the *Sequoian*. I kept copies of all editions with ads for Cici's Vintage Clothing and made notes on their relative success. An article might suggest a motive for Penn's murder, or at the very least, remind me of recent developments in our community. I didn't expect much success, but I couldn't think of anything else to do until evening relieved me from store duties.

The mail carrier dropped off a larger than usual pile of orders. I logged onto my computer. Sales over the weekend had rendered my Web site outdated; most of the pictured items had sold, and I needed to update the information. The challenge of matching clothing to customers gave me great satisfaction. It was also time to check out estate sales and secondhand clothing stores. With parties requiring guests to wear costumes, and with the upcoming Christmas season, I hoped that people would remain eager to buy from me.

Next, I checked my favorite stocks. My interest in the stock market started in high school, when I tracked the market price of the *Herald* for an economics class. My nest egg was growing nicely.

While I was on the Internet, I decided to check out the *Herald* Web site. Ads placed in the electronic version of the newspaper worked well when I wanted to sell outside of the door-to-door delivery area. Checking for headlines electronically would keep me from getting ink on my pretty pink dress. I confess that I felt as dainty and fresh as a spring flower when I wore that dress, my waist cinched small enough to make me feel like Scarlet O'Hara.

But what was I looking for? Suzanne said Penn was pursuing a big story. I decided to start with the current date and work back until something caught my attention. *If* something caught my attention.

Soon I fell into a rhythm of scanning headlines and reading an occasional abstract. If needed, I could look up the entire article in my newspaper file. News of plans for the Land Run festivities filled recent issues. A week ago, Ron Grace won the mayoral election in a landslide against his Democratic opponent. In the same issue, he announced his plans to invite the mayors of Grace City, North Dakota, and Grace, Idaho, to the upcoming festival. They must have declined; I hadn't seen any visiting dignitaries. Then again, after the gunfight, I didn't notice much of anything.

Thinking of the mayoral race reminded me of the

primary election for city officials in May, the only vote that mattered in local politics. No Democrat had won since FDR had left office. Ron was opposed in his bid for reelection by Jordan Malcolm, the big name in Grace Gulch realty and a distant Grace cousin. If I remembered correctly, the *Herald* had come out in support of Mr. Malcolm. I searched by subjects "primary election" and "Jordan Malcolm" to find relevant articles.

The first Sunday issue in May had run articles in support of candidates from each party. The paper had to make a pretense of nonpartisan support. The Democratic candidate—the lawyer who handled most of my legal affairs, Georgia Hafferty—ran unopposed. Penn had written a fairly objective statement of her experience and successes, as well as her unpopular stands on issues, from public land management to hydroelectric power.

Penn surprised the town by endorsing Ron Grace's opponent, Jordan Malcolm, as the Republican candidate for mayor. He pointed to Malcolm's strong business sense and described him as a good man to lead Grace Gulch into the future. He criticized Ron's "provincial" mentality and poked fun at the "Grace-filled" map that adorned the mayor's office. Pushpins marked the locations of various members of the Grace clan, as well as institutions and communities named after Grace. Penn pointed out the possible conflict of church and state and wondered aloud that someone hadn't filed a suit against the city. He didn't make any friends with that article, I decided.

I didn't remember how the *Sequoian* had handled the primaries, so I switched Web sites.

The difference between the papers was immediately obvious. News items about school events at Lizzy Gaynor Elementary and a weekly column by Pastor Waldberg from the Gaynor-founded Word of Truth Fellowship indicated its pro-Gaynor roots. Aside from that, it provided more balanced coverage than the *Herald*. Mitch supported reelecting Mayor Ron. He ran our town with a mixture of common sense and humanity, in spite of occasional silly stunts (my words, not his). I guess Gaynor figured Ron was the best of the Grace-tied candidates; Georgia was the only candidate not related to the Graces.

After spending most of the morning on the computer, I decided that if Penn was on the trail of a story, he hadn't written about it in the paper. I didn't catch a sniff of anything controversial. The primary coverage came the closest, but the mayor won reelection in spite of Penn's opposition. So that didn't count as a motive, did it?

I turned off the monitor and closed my eyes. I should at least talk with the mayor, however. How could I snag an interview? Our paths didn't cross all that often. Perhaps his cousin Cord could pave the way. Poor Cord. I wondered if Reiner had continued his harassment. One thing was certain: He had not arrested Cord yet. If that happened, I would hear before he reached the police station.

After a sack lunch, I cleaned my hands and prepared the mail orders. The Fed Ex driver stopped by around three. After much persuasion, I had convinced him to stop in Grace Gulch at least every other day. The company didn't like him to wander too far from I-44 and Route 66, and our town was nestled in the hills of Lincoln County, well off the beaten path.

A constant stream of customers kept me busy for the remainder of the afternoon. A brief flurry came after five and purchased most of the remaining special Land Run items. Time for a sale? Not yet, I decided. As soon as the cloud still hanging over Cord and Dina disappeared, I would close for a few days and shop for new stock. Then I would hold a sale for any holdovers from the festival. Promptly at six, I turned the sign to CLOSED and walked out the back door to my car.

At home, I exchanged my dress for a robe before starting supper. I boiled pasta shells and made an indulgent sauce out of Velveeta and cream cheese, then placed the casserole in the oven on low heat while I headed to the shower. My hair got wet, but I put off styling it until the morning, after I decided what to wear. For one night I could let it go to seed. That's what I called it, anyhow, because left untended, my washed-out hair looked like a dandelion gone to seed. I pulled on my favorite OU sweatshirt, faded and spotted from the paint job on my first apartment, and blue jeans with holes. I didn't intend to think about work or investigations for the next twelve hours. Maybe I could catch up on the ladies' Bible study I had decided to join at church, and then perhaps watch a half-hour comedy on television.

I had tossed a salad reminiscent of Jenna's California

dish—I had enjoyed the A and A combination and decided to recreate it at home—when the doorbell rang. I peeked out the front window. Audie. Oh, no! I opened the door an inch. "What's up?"

"I was driving by and, well, I wondered if you had eaten dinner yet."

"Actually, I've got a casserole in the oven."

Audie looked disappointed.

I sighed. "Why don't you join me?"

"I thought you'd never ask." Audie walked through my front door, not reacting to my disheveled appearance. I added an extra place setting to the table and headed for my bedroom to change back into my dress. I looked at my reflection in the mirror. As expected, my hair sprang in a dozen directions. I ran a comb through it to get out the worst of the snarls but decided to leave on my casual clothes. *This is the real me*, I decided. If last night meant anything, if there was to be a future for Audie and me, he would have to accept me at my worst as well as at my best. And damp, frizzy hair, paint-stained sweatshirt, and holey jeans definitely fell into the "worst" category. Besides, the damage had been done. He'd already seen me at the door.

A couple of minutes passed before I returned downstairs. Audie had gone out to the front porch swing, a hiss that was his version of whistling issuing from between his lips.

"It's a beautiful night," he said. "Can supper wait while you join me for a few minutes?"

"Sure." *Coward*, I told myself. Outside maybe he

wouldn't notice how bad I looked. Moonlight added magic to everything. I slid into the swing—the selling point for the house, as far as I was concerned—and settled into the crook of Audie's arm.

"Careful." He handed me a bouquet redolent of Oklahoma—baby's breath and daises, lilies and Indian paintbrush. "I asked for the flowers that Bob Grace described in his letters."

Tears came to my eyes. "They're beautiful."

He pecked me on the cheek. "Don't want to give the neighbors too much to talk about," he whispered in my ear. Then he straightened up and held me against his shoulder, and we swung in silence for a few minutes. It was a clear night, and the starry host made my small worries seem no bigger than a grain of sand.

"I figure the stars haven't changed since Bob Grace first set eyes on this place," Audie said. "I can locate Orion's belt and know he saw the same constellations." He paused. "Minus the streetlights, of course. I sometimes wonder what it would be like to experience total darkness, without any lights shining except for the heavens."

"I suppose I came as close to that as anyone does in this day and age, growing up on a ranch. It took me awhile to get used to city noises—well, you know what I mean. The occasional rumble of a train. Cars passing. Instead of crickets and roosters and cows."

"It gives you perspective, I guess. 'I was there when he set the heavens in place, when he marked out the horizon on the face of the deep, when he established the clouds above and fixed securely the fountains of the deep.' Solomon described wisdom as being present at Creation." Of course Audie could quote the right proverb.

"We could use some of that wisdom with this mess." I summarized my day's investigation. "The only hint of a motive I found concerns Mayor Grace. Penn supported Malcolm. But the mayor won reelection in spite of the opposition. So why should he care? And I can't imagine him murdering someone."

"None of them seem like a credible suspect," Audie reminded me.

That was the core of the problem. While I knew in my heart of hearts that neither Dina nor Cord committed murder, I didn't want to believe that anybody I had known my entire life had done it either. Maybe that's why I latched onto Suzanne as a suspect. She was a newcomer to Grace Gulch. The possibility left me cold, and I shivered.

"I've kept you outside too long. Let's go inside." Audie held my hand as we crossed the porch and then opened the door like a gentleman. Light splashed out, casting shadows across the wooden boards. I saw the porcupine outline of my head, and remembered my unkempt appearance. I hurried inside.

"All I have is some macaroni and cheese and a salad," I said once we entered the living room.

"That's almost a honeymooner's delight."

I lifted my eyebrows.

"You know, honeymoon salad, lettuce alone."

I smiled to let him know I understood the play on

words: let us alone.

He grinned at his corny joke. He sniffed the air. "It smells good."

I looked down at my paint-stained shirt and holey jeans and drew in a deep breath. "Okay. Why don't you get our drinks ready—I'll take some hot chocolate, it's in the cupboard—while I dress for dinner." I had changed my mind.

"Change your clothes?" Audie wrinkled his nose. "Why?"

I blushed. "I'm not exactly dressed for company."

Audie turned me around to face him. "Cecilia Wilde, you are beautiful just as you are. Don't you dare change on me." He reached out a hand to touch my dandelion hair. "I like the hair. I like the look. I like you." He leaned in and kissed me, a gentle touch that feathered warmth on my lips, one that lingered and shattered me inside. My arms stole around his neck as I returned his kiss. Stars danced in my head, and I was Cinderella, with the feeling that "the room had no ceiling or floor."

Audie broke off the kiss and backed away, still holding onto my hands. "I never knew it could be like this." He brushed my cheek with his fingers. "I want more—much more—but not now. A few other things need to happen first." He drew in a deep breath. "Like a wedding."

Cinderella-like, the room twirled. Did Audie use the word wedding? Was this a proposal? Or was he indicating his adherence to biblical standards regarding the sanctity of the marriage bed? In either case, my worries about Audie's possible interest in Suzanne or Jenna subsided. Audie was a godly man, someone I could trust.

I gazed into velvet blue eyes and wondered if the same stars danced in mine. He looked great, a dark cardigan a perfect match for neatly pressed corduroy pants. His hair smelled like wood shavings. I wanted to fling myself into his arms again. Instead, I forced myself to step back.

"At least let me go splash water on my face." I smiled, as shy as a girl on her first date.

"And I'll fix the hot chocolate," he said, walking toward the kitchen.

I didn't change, but I did spray on lily of the valley perfume before I returned. The teakettle sang merrily in time with Audie's whistling as he stirred two mugs of hot chocolate. The macaroni and cheese bubbled on the table, and tongs lay beside the salad bowl.

"May I return thanks?" Audie asked after we sat down. I nodded. "Heavenly Father, thank You for this meal. More than that, I thank You for Cici. For her hard work. For her kind heart and inner and outer beauty that shines through whatever she wears. Give us Your wisdom as we try to learn the truth about Penn's death."

Warmth hugged me, and it wasn't from the oven.

For the next few minutes, we dug into the food and didn't say much. "Mmm, this is creamy. Care to share your secret?" Audie dished out a second serving of macaroni.

"It's just Velveeta and cream cheese, milk and butter. I call it my busy day special. Enid Waldberg passed the recipe among the church ladies."

"Another feather to add to your cap," Audie said. "And this salad is great. Suspiciously familiar, in fact."

I felt heat rise in my cheeks. "I decided that I liked Jenna's salad recipe."

"Good idea." He speared lettuce and an Ariane apple on his fork. "You don't have to prove anything. Not to me. Not to anyone else. You're nothing like your sisters. God made you the way you are—unique. Special. Beautiful. You don't have to pretend to be someone else." Then a smile creased his cheeks. "Although you look fetching in your costumes."

Audie wheeled his way past my defenses and pointed the finger at my deep-seated insecurities. "Oh, but I do have something to prove. I spent my life on a ranch, but I never wanted to be a rancher's wife, not even as a little girl. Then Mom died and Jenna left home and I took over running the house when I was thirteen. Everyone assumes that I love ranch life." Even Cord. Especially Cord. "But I don't. I got away for a couple of years, and now I've escaped as far as town. My business is about as different from ranching as you can get. But sometimes I feel like Jenna is living the life I wanted."

"It's not the ranch you love." Audie set down his fork. "It's the people. And the community."

"Yes." The word pushed past my teeth in a gush of breath. How could this man, who had known me for only a few months, understand me so well?

"And now we have to solve Penn's murder to return Grace Gulch to happier days."

My heart leapt at his use of "we."

"Yes, we do." I agreed, in every sense of the word.

13

September 19, 1891 Excerpt B

You have heard of the Boomers and the Sooners. The Boomer movement is fading. They accomplished their purpose by forcing the government to make the lands available to white settlement. I suppose they achieved individual glory in the same proportion as the rest of us, and many of them wait at the border by my side, hoping for a second chance.

Sooners still abound. There is a heavy presence of marshals to prevent premature entry into the Indian lands. Some of the marshals are women, who look rather odd in their sidesaddles and skirts while holding a rifle as steady as an Indian scout.

Even so, I am sorely tempted to become a Sooner myself. I want our land so badly that I am ready to cheat to earn it. I have found a cave near the gulch where I can hide until the noon hour has passed. Then I could join in the run—just farther ahead of anyone else.

Tuesday, September 24

"Last night's revelations disturbed me more than I care to admit," I confessed to Audie while I was loading the dishwasher after dinner. "I wanted to believe that Grace won the race fair and square."

"So you've decided that the letters aren't connected to Penn's death?"

Trust Audie to hit the nail on the head. I shrugged uncomfortably.

"I don't know. I don't see how they could be." Unless the mayor wanted to protect the Grace family name.

"Do you think the mayor resented Penn's support of his opponent?"

"Not enough to kill him!" The vehemence of my retort surprised even me. "After all, Penn supported his campaign after he won the primary."

"But if you mix in a possible scandal involving the town's sacred history?" The question hung in midair.

"I can't imagine that Mayor Ron would kill somebody in cold blood." That lay at the heart of my objections. I voted for Ron Grace ever since my first election. I liked the man and thought he did a good job for our little town.

Audie sighed. He ticked off the names. "Do you think Gwen Hardy is capable of murder? Suzanne? Mitch Gaynor? We know Dina didn't do it."

I squirmed in my seat. He was right.

"The murderer is going to be someone you know." The compassion on Audie's face just about did me in. "We have to be objective. We can't let our emotions get in the way. 'The truth is rarely pure and never simple.' Wilde understood the paradoxical nature of truth. It doesn't stand alone. The murder didn't occur in a vacuum."

That was the problem. I wanted the murder to separate itself from my everyday life and the people I knew. But it did not occur in a vacuum, and the sooner I accepted that and moved forward, the better off I'd be. How much better it was to identify the killer and see him, or her, of course, brought to justice, than for a cloud of suspicion to hang over a group of people. Especially when that group included my sister. I blotted out my feelings and considered the facts we had uncovered.

"I admit that the mayor had a couple of reasons to dislike Penn. Not supporting him in the mayoral race—I don't think that's enough of a motive for murder. But rewriting the history of the land run. . .I just don't know."

"Let's clean up in here and then talk about it some more." Audie helped me load the dishwasher. "How about a fire tonight?"

The fall evening had a chilly edge, and I agreed. Soon flames leapt up the chimney. Each hiss and crackle spat another question into my mind.

"If only I knew someone at the *Herald*. Knew them well, I mean."

Audie slanted me a suspicious glance. "Why?"

"I keep wondering what the story was that Penn mentioned to Suzanne."

"You don't think it was the Grace papers?"

"No." I shook my head. "Because Penn didn't run the story."

"Do you think he might have tried blackmail—"

I shook my head even before Audie could finish his thought.

"Think about it." Audie continued to press his point. "Penn told Suzanne that he needed money. Maybe he thought the mayor was an easy mark."

"It wasn't in Penn's character. He was a newsman first. Biased, yes, and not exactly Pulitzer Prize material. But if he thought he had the goods on the land run, he would have run the story. Whatever story he was working on involved something else."

Audie leaned forward and poked at the log with the fire tongs. Sparks hissed in the air. "If it's a local story—which seems likely—the *Sequoian* could be pursuing the same leads. And you do know an insider there."

I heard the smile in his voice. "Dina! But if she knew anything related to the murder, she would have told us."

"But she may not realize the significance of what she knows. If she knows anything."

"If she knows something. . ." Fear tightened the vise on my throat, and my voice squeaked through the tiny airhole. "She's in danger! Let her stay blissfully ignorant."

But blindness wouldn't guarantee her safety. If the murderer thought Dina knew something, she remained in danger. Worse than that, she worked for Mitch Gaynor, the only suspect we hadn't interviewed yet, along with the mayor. Why had Dina decided to major in journalism and apply for an internship with the town newspaper?

"Talk to her again," Audie said. "Ask her what she knows about stories that didn't make it into print."

I reached for the phone on the end table—I confess that I stayed with an old-fashioned, olive green model for my living room at least—and dialed Dina's number.

"Yo, Cic," she answered on the second ring. The joys of caller ID. Loud pounding of the press in full run almost drowned out her voice. "Let me go to the break room and call you back. I can't hear when the presses are running."

My phone rang a few minutes later. I explained the situation. "We're looking for any unpublished stories, especially anything involving the Hardys, Suzanne Jay, or the mayor."

"Sure. I have an appointment with Mitch tomorrow, you know, a review, when he looks at what I've done this summer and what more I want to learn. I'll ask him about it then."

"That might not be such a good idea. He's one of our potential suspects."

"Don't worry! I can, you know, act, and he won't guess a thing." She giggled. "Look, I'd better get back to work before somebody fusses at me for being on the phone."

"It's late," Audie said after I'd hung up. "We'd better call it a night." He reached out a hand and brushed his fingers against my hair. "I like this look. Wear it again sometime."

Wow. I hadn't thought about my "natural" appearance since before supper. I patted down the ends. "If you say so." No matter how much Audie professed to like the look, I didn't feel comfortable with the flyaway state of my hair.

"I do." He kissed me briefly on the lips, a promise of things to come. "See you tomorrow?"

"I'll call when I hear from Dina."

"Au revoir, then." With a nod of his head, Audie let himself out the front door.

—

Dina stopped by the store on her way to work on Wednesday afternoon. I locked the door behind my last customer and took her to my office.

"I have an assignment!" Dina saw herself as the Lois Lane of Grace Gulch, ready for Superman to appear and sweep her away. "Mitch wants me to cover the PTA beat."

I let her describe her ideas of unique angles for the story in excruciating detail. At last, she wound down. That's when I asked, "Did you learn anything about stories that weren't published?"

"No. Not about anybody you mentioned, or anyone I remember seeing close to the action." Her voice rose in contrast to her negative answer.

"Tone it down." When excited, her voice grew loud enough to carry through walls. Anyone walking by my office window could hear, and now more than ever discretion was key. "There is no need to tell the whole town your news."

"How's this then?" she whispered. "There is something fishy going on. You remember how I ran the printing press by myself last week?"

I nodded. How could I forget? She arrived at the

store with ink-stained hands and smeared some of the Land Run merchandise, causing a lot of extra work. Her excitement at seeing her words appear in bold type on paper bubbled over onto me, and I couldn't stay upset with her.

"I double-checked the circulation run listed on the front page—'cause it seemed weird, the population of Grace Gulch is only 2,000 and that includes families, you know, but the circulation is listed as 2,500. So I loaded enough paper for 2,500 copies."

"Hyperbole, maybe." I wondered what circulation the *Herald* boasted.

"The printer came out and yelled at me. Asked me what I thought I was doing, wasting all that paper, we only needed 1,500 copies." Dina pouted, the same expression on her face that she used to get her way with Dad. She looked like a naughty child.

"It sounds like an honest mistake," I said. Although almost doubling the real circulation numbers stretched hyperbole past believability. "Maybe they run 2,500 copies for the Sunday edition or something."

"He acted like he was going to take the extra cost out of my paycheck. I mean, I checked the records before I started. Every day it says they print 2,500 copies. How was I supposed to know that they only needed 1,500 this one time?" She bounced in the chair and tucked a knee under her.

"Wait a minute. You mean that the records indicate that they print 2,500 all the time?"

"That's what I've been trying to tell you." She twisted her face as if to say, You can be so dumb. "And there's more." Her voice trilled on the last word, a ghostly whisper. "I worked with the bookkeeper last week."

"Oh?" I bet that didn't last long. Dina didn't get along with numbers. She needed a calculator to add one plus one.

"She was working on accounts payable. And there were tons of overdue notices. I mean, everything was at least a month overdue."

I glanced at the pile of bills on my desk and wondered if they constituted a "ton" in Dina's mind. "Maybe she pays the bills once a month. That's what I do. Sometimes payments and overdue notices cross in the mail."

"Man, I'm not talking about a late payment notice. I mean, like, dun letters saying 'no more deliveries if you don't pay immediately.' "

Now that surprised me. The *Sequoian* was a Grace Gulch institution. It shouldn't have that degree of financial trouble.

"So I wonder if someone is cooking the books." Dina announced it like a foregone conclusion. "That, or the bookkeeper is really bad at her job."

"Or they can't afford to pay their bills." Which seemed unlikely.

"Maybe that's why they hired me." Dina laughed with a toss of her head. "Double the work for half the money. That's what interns are good for." She turned serious. "Do you want me to spy it out?"

"Definitely not." Too dangerous, but I wouldn't say that to my sister. That would ensure her plunging into the most turbulent waters.

She pouted. "I'll keep my ears and eyes open."

"Don't you have a term paper to write or something?"

She laughed at me. "Not until the end of the semester. Last-minute Lucy, that's me."

We finished sharing our lunch—a turkey club sandwich, Gaynor Goodies' daily lunch special—when someone banged on the front door. I ignored the sound. Couldn't they read the Closed sign? A few minutes later, the knocking renewed on the back door.

"I'd better see who it is."

"I'll get it." Dina swallowed the last bite of her sandwich with a Red Bull and went to the back door. She returned in a minute. "Look who the cat dragged in."

"I couldn't stay away." Audie grinned at me. Warm feelings welled inside of me, which had nothing to do with the coffee I held in my hand. We gawked at each other like teenagers at the prom.

Dina looked from one of us to the other. "Should I leave?" A smirk curled the edges of her shocking red lips.

"No," I said.

"That's not necessary," Audie said at the same time.

Heat rose in my cheeks, revealing my feelings more clearly than if I had spoken them out loud, but Audie pretended not to notice.

"In fact, I'm glad that you're here." Audie spoke to Dina "This concerns you, too."

Foreboding dampened my spirits. That meant he had news about the investigation. And it involved

Dina, the one person I most wanted to protect.

"It's about the guns. The props we used in the play."

"Was Cord's gun the murder weapon? I don't believe it." Dina's cheerful facade dropped for a moment, and she looked like a worried little girl afraid to show Daddy her bad report card. "That's—"

"No, that's not the problem." Audie interrupted her. "That is, I don't know the details of the ballistics report or if they even have it yet. It's something else."

"What is it?" My anxiety burst the words out.

"I went over everything we did with those guns, to be sure my memory was accurate. Frontier guns are hardly my specialty. We decided to use the real thing—"

"—because too many people would complain if you substituted a modern weapon." Dina nodded. "And the mayor offered to let us use guns from his collection. He has some cool stuff, a flintlock rifle and Winchesters. That sort of thing."

"And you. . ." Audie looked in my direction. "You and Cord figured out which weapons would have been used in the gunfight."

"The Colt model 1892. Cord had given Bob Grace's gun to the mayor for a Christmas present." I didn't like the direction Audie's questions had taken. It felt like a police interrogation, only the tables had turned. Dina and I were the bad guys, and Audie was the detective hot on our trail.

"So the mayor had Bob Grace's original Colt—in prime condition, according to him—and several others of similar vintage. And he offered to loan three of them to us, in case something went wrong with one of them. Three, not two, right?"

"Yeah. I kept them locked up at the MGM." Dina's facade slipped back into place, pleased at the memory of the confidence Audie had shown in her. "Cord, Penn, and I test fired them a week before the festival. They all worked."

"And they both took the guns home after our last practice. And after the. . .incident, the police bagged both of those guns." Audie's face reflected his distaste of the memory.

"That's the way I remember it." I recalled the look of shocked disbelief on Cord's face, the way the gun had slipped out of his fingers into the evidence bag in Reiner's waiting hand.

"But they didn't know about the third gun? They didn't take it?" Audie asked.

"They asked me where the guns came from, and I told them. I don't think I mentioned the extra gun. Why should I? We didn't use it in the play." Dina shrugged. "I haven't checked the gun case since Saturday. Maybe I should have, but I couldn't put the guns back until the police finished with them. They weren't props anymore. They were evidence—" She pronounced the *i* with an *ee* sound—"in a murder investigation. I didn't want to think about it." The worried little girl tone returned to her voice.

Audie's questions began to make horrible sense. "Why?" I demanded. "What's wrong?"

"I checked the gun case when I thought about it

this morning, when I was putting away some of the other props." Audie's face set into grim lines, the hint of wrinkles marring his pale forehead. "It was empty. The third gun is missing."

September 19, 1891 Excerpt C

When I rode out yesterday, searching for the cave, Gaynor followed me from town. He as much as accused me of cheating. For a moment, I wanted to challenge him to a duel for the insult. But then I thought of you and our future, and I relented.

He told me that he has pointed me out to the marshals as a troublemaker, and that any move I make will be closely watched. After he left, I found the cave in a perfect spot, hidden by leafy sycamore trees. I wonder if I can escape the marshals' attention long enough to return to the spot before Tuesday.

I wonder about Gaynor's motives. Maybe he is also seeking a way to speed his race. I sense that you are disappointed in me, but I will do whatever I must to secure our future.

Your loving fiancé,
Robert Grace

Wednesday, September 25

"The third gun is missing?" Dina repeated. "But that's impossible. I was very careful with the keys." Her hair fluffed out like a rooster's hackles, preparing my sister to take offence against any accusation of failing to do her duty. For all her rebellious style, she was a responsible young woman. She never missed a day's work or flunked a class.

"I know you were." Audie jingled the keys in his pocket. "But I had a second set, and I kept them at the office. Somebody might have borrowed them, or made a copy, or something."

"But that's. . ." Dina's lip trembled. "That's terrible. Have either one of you read the paper this morning?"

I shook my head. Yesterday's immersion in news would last me for a while.

"Not yet," Audie said. "I went straight to the theater."

"Look at this." Dina shoved the *Herald* at us. "I have to keep up with the competition."

Penn's murder remained on page 1—the *Herald* would keep it there until the case was solved and the murderer sentenced—and today's headline screamed: HARDY SHOT WITH VINTAGE GUN.

"Does it mention the murder weapon?" Audie asked over my shoulder.

I scanned the paragraphs. "It doesn't say. But the police are sure that Hardy was shot by a Colt revolver—"

"—Probably a model 1892," Dina finished for me. "The same kind we used in the play."

The three of us looked at each other. With all the guns in our part of the world, why didn't the murderer choose a more modern weapon?

"They're going to suspect me again. Me and Cord." Dina kept her tone light, but I could tell that the cloud of suspicion bothered her. "It was one of our guns. You know it was. It must have been."

"There's no need to jump to conclusions," Audie said. He used the kind of soothing voice that worked with babies. I could have told him that it wouldn't work on my sister. "It says here that the police have sent the weapons used in the reenactment to the crime lab in Oklahoma City for further testing. It sounds like they don't have a match for the murder weapon yet."

I could have warned him that logic probably wouldn't work with Dina either.

"But don't you see? People are going to talk. They're going to say, 'I wonder what revolver they used in the play. That Wilde girl must know something about it.'"

"No one is going to think that," Audie said. He held the paper and read the article for himself, as if hoping the contents would change.

"Hah! You don't know small towns. That's exactly what they're going to say." Dina sniffed.

The rumor mill wouldn't stop there. I hoped Dina could see that. "They're also going to be asking each other, 'Don't you have your grandfather's old Colt? What model was it?' The next time I stop in at Gaynor Goodies, Jessie will have a more accurate listing of all the model 1892s in existence in Grace Gulch than if the tax assessor took an inventory. It's not all that unique."

Dina glared at me, challenging my logic.

"I've noticed that people here hang on to old guns

and farm implements the way some people refurbish classic cars." Audie grinned. "Half the towns in Lincoln County have a historical society, and the most popular item after period clothing"—he nodded at me—"any clothing Cici hasn't laid her hands on, that is—seems to be old guns."

"Think of Mayor Ron's office. You've seen that special case over his desk where he keeps Bob Grace's original gun." Every tour of the town hall ended at the mayor's office, and the gun case drew all eyes. That, and all the memorabilia he had collected from other Grace cities.

Dina stomped her foot. "But no one cares about everybody else's guns. Not even the mayor's guns, because we borrowed them for the play, and he didn't take part. A Colt model 1892—one that I handled and that I vetted for use—did shoot Penn Hardy. And now we know that a Colt model 1892 killed him. Ergo, I supplied the gun, and Cord shot the one that killed Penn Hardy."

Audie cleared his throat to protest.

"Okay, okay. The same model of gun that killed him. Big difference." Dina wandered into the front room and came back with the doughnut holes I had bought at Gaynor Goodies that morning. "These are delicious. You should get them more often." She swallowed three of them whole. "I've got class in half an hour. See you later." She crammed headphones over her ears, her head already bobbing before she shut the door behind her. Maybe her favorite Christian music would soothe her spirits where our words had failed.

"I have to talk with the mayor." I couldn't put it off any longer. Ever since his name appeared on our list of suspects, I had dreaded the idea of questioning the most powerful man in our town. Even if he was Cord's cousin and a lovable eccentric.

"Him, and Mitch Gaynor." Audie rolled up the newspaper and drummed the table with it. "I can get away again tomorrow morning. Does that work for you?"

Knowing Audie intended to come with me made my insides wiggle like a happy puppy. "The city offices open at nine. I can come in to work late."

"Good." Audie looked up the phone number in the slim city directory I kept behind the cash register and called for an appointment. "Nine tomorrow morning. Thanks. We'll be there." He hung up the phone, rapped the edge of the desk with his fingers, and frowned. "I was hoping that Dina had checked the gun boxes after the play. Maybe she had already returned the third gun to the mayor. That would have been the simplest solution."

"Yes. But—"

"Now two of his weapons are in police custody. I don't know how long they hold on to things like that. Until the case goes to trial?"

"Probably. And now the other gun has disappeared. He'll rue the day he agreed to lend us anything. He might turn the blame on us, you know."

"Hmm?" Audie scrubbed his hand over his jaw.

"Like all good politicians do, to wiggle out of a tight spot. He might say that if we hadn't come up with this harebrained scheme to reenact the gunfight, no one would have died. And his guns wouldn't be involved in a homicide." If the mayor said that, he'd be blaming Audie even more than me. Tears threatened to spill out. "Somehow the blame always seems to fall on me or someone I. . .care about." Did I almost use the word love? It was far too soon.

"I won't let that happen. This time you have me." Audie lifted my chin with one long, slender finger and looked into my eyes, his eyes as clear as our city lake, hints of forever in their depths.

"All right." My fears faded away. This man would direct the next few days as effectively as he staged a play. "All's well that ends well."

"That's my girl. Of course you're scared of thinking the worst of people you know. Wilde said, 'The reason we all like to think so well of others is that we are all afraid for ourselves. The basis for optimism is sheer terror.' "

Oscar Wilde again. Who else would Audie quote to lighten the mood? I really needed to rediscover the playwright. I searched my limited knowledge. "Dorian Gray?"

"That's it."

"I have to admit that he has a point. Again."

"But after all, we have God on our side, and whom shall we fear?"

"Hey, not fair, now you're quoting from the Psalms. Even I know that one. Psalm 27." Our music director had sung an unforgettable rendition of the lyrics more than once. The thunderous refrain echoed in my mind and I relaxed. "The Lord is my light and my salvation.

He will show the way."

"That's the spirit."

I stayed busy for the remainder of the day, but that didn't prevent me from thinking about the investigation. Which gun killed Penn? Was it one of the guns borrowed for the play? *Don't think about that now, you've got new customers to add to your client list.* I grabbed the guest register from the weekend—almost full after only one weekend's business—and added new names to my growing database of potential customers.

Who took the third gun? I updated my accounting files with recent shipments and printed out monthly statements. I couldn't pay bills if I didn't get paid.

Is the Sequoian *in financial trouble? And if it is, does it have anything to do with Penn's murder?* If so, the connection didn't seem obvious. I added recent bills to my tickler file and wrote out checks for those due within the next week.

Cord called midafternoon. "What's this I hear about a missing prop gun?"

I should have known. The grapevine didn't need listening devices to keep up with the latest news. It plucked information out of thin air.

"Reiner came around to ask me about it," Cord explained.

So Audie must have told the police about his discovery.

"What does he think? That I had both guns in my holster and shot two-handed? Even my great-grandfather didn't pretend to do that." His voice softened. "Not that I know of."

"A gun is missing." I twirled the phone cord while

we talked. "Please don't add to the rumor mill. Audie and I are going to talk with Mayor Ron tomorrow morning and explain the situation." And ask some questions, but Cord didn't need to know that.

"I want to come with you."

"That's not a good idea." The last time Cord met Audie face-to-face, they pecked at each other like roosters. If that happened again, we wouldn't get a thing out of the mayor.

"If you say so." Cord must have heard about all the time I spent with Audie this week, and my refusal probably felt like a rejection. I didn't like to hurt him— he was a good friend—but I wasn't sure what to do.

"Why don't we get together some time this weekend, and I'll tell you everything that I've learned so far."

"It's a date." Cord sounded positively cheerful as he accepted my alternative and hung up.

Customers came and went until it was time to close up shop. The Word of Truth's Wednesday night Bible study and prayer meeting kept me occupied for a couple of hours. After that, I puttered around the house, vacuuming the living room floor, and decided to call it an early night about nine thirty.

As usual, I headed for my closet to decide what to wear the next day. *Cecilia Wilde, you are beautiful just as you are. Don't you dare change on me.* Audie's words ricocheted through my body, spreading warmth from head to toe in its path. I giggled. Even so, a paint-stained OU shirt wasn't appropriate office wear. I dressed to please myself and to model my product.

I chose a pair of purple bell-bottom slacks that would slide well over black leather boots, a tie-dyed long-sleeved shirt, and multicolored beads. I could leave my hair in its flyaway state for my '60s look. Which coat? I grinned. My trench coat, of course. It didn't quite match the '60s-style, but it fit in with my detective plans for the day.

—

The doorbell rang at half past eight the following morning. Audie. I rushed to open the door. He hunched his shoulders against the predicted rain that splashed on the ground, turning the red dirt into mud.

"Good morning, Detective Wilde." He grinned at my trench coat. "You're looking good. If you don't mind, I thought we could drive to the city offices in your car. My windshield wipers need to be replaced." He hung up his windbreaker on my coat rack and headed for my desk. "I thought we should take Bob Grace's letter we found with us. Ask the mayor if Penn had shown it to him."

The doorbell rang again, startling me. Who else would come to my house at this early hour? I looked out my peephole. Cord. Oh, no. I couldn't leave him outside in the rain, so I opened the door. "Come in."

"Howe! I thought I would find you here." Cord removed his Stetson and hung it on the coat tree, rain drops clinging to his springing golden curls. "I wanted to catch you both before you take off for Ron's office. I know you too well, Cici. You're going there to question him about the guns. I can't believe you're seriously considering my cousin as a murderer." He cocked his elbows at an angle to his waist, poster boy of belligerence.

Audie and I looked at each other. He shrugged. *This one is up to you.*

I plunged ahead. "The mayor was in an ideal place to see what happened."

"And if he saw anything, anything at all, he's already told the police about it. They did question him, you know. Reiner couldn't resist the opportunity to grill one of the Graces." Cord's chin jutted out, his Adam's apple bobbing up and down. He gestured at my trench coat. "This is just like you. You think you're a Samantha Spade and that all you have to do is talk to people and they'll tell you things they never mentioned to the police."

My face flamed. Audie had referred to my detective getup as well, but he made it a compliment.

"Just a minute, Grace." Audie spoke for the first time since Cord entered the house. "Cici is asking questions because you and Dina are both under suspicion. Don't you get it? She's trying to help you. Somebody killed Penn Hardy, and your cousin is one of the people in the right place to make the shot."

Cord took a step toward Audie.

"Don't you see?" I stood between the two men. This was worse than I feared. "We have to talk with the mayor, if only to eliminate him."

"And I trust Cici," Audie continued as if I hadn't spoken. "To follow the truth, wherever it leads. Now, if you don't mind, we have a nine o'clock appointment." He opened the door and gestured for Cord to leave.

Cord looked at me one last long moment. "I hope you know what you're doing." He jammed his Stetson back on his head and walked through the door. We followed him.

Once inside the car, I flicked on the heater, although I felt fine. Audie had championed me, and it warmed me to my toes. But only heat would defog the car windows.

"Thanks for taking your car today." He spoke as if nothing special had happened, as if he hadn't stood up for me to a prime alpha male.

"No problem." We drove the short distance to the city office building, rebuilt at the edge of town for the millennium.

"Do you know why Grace Gulch doesn't have a town square? You know, court and jail and all that in the center of town?"

"Save that for your county seats. No, we're just small potatoes here. We don't even have our own jail." We found a parking place and dashed inside.

Ron's secretary, Betty Bruner, greeted us at the door with her high-pitched squeal. The shapely blond provided the town's only competition to Suzanne Jay's come-hither looks. "I'm sorry, you can't see Mayor Grace just now. He has a visitor."

"A visitor? We have a nine o'clock appointment," I protested. Now that I had mustered the courage to come, I didn't want it to seep away while we waited.

"The gentleman came in with the mayor this

morning. I'm sure it will be just a few minutes."

I wanted to ask about the mayor's unexpected visitor but decided against it. Girlish voice and sexy appearance aside, Betty did a good job and kept the mayor's business affairs in order and as secret as they could be in a small town.

Soon the murmur of voices behind the door grew to a dull roar.

"That sounds like—" Audie began.

"Mitch Gaynor." I had recognized the voice at the same time.

We stared at each other. What a stroke of luck. The two suspects we had not yet questioned were at the same place at the same time, and more than that, appeared to be having a serious disagreement. I wanted to creep closer to the door to hear better. While I considered the wisdom of such a move, Betty appeared in front of us.

"You look cold. I brought you some fresh coffee."

That settled it. I couldn't sneak around with a cup of hot java in my hand.

Mayor Ron's voice rose to a bellow. The three of us turned our heads as words exploded through the closed door. "Repeat that. . .dead man. . ."

Repeat what? What had Mitch said? The mayor's threat echoed the argument between the original Grace and Gaynor at the time of the land run.

Different sounds replaced shouts. A crash, the sound of glass breaking, followed by a thud, then a crack loud enough to shatter my eardrums.

Betty sprang to the door.

"Call 911!" Audie barked at her and pushed past her into the mayor's office.

The glass of the gun case holding Bob Grace's gun was shattered, the velvet lining empty. Gaynor and Grace faced each other like duelers at high noon, shock mirrored on both faces.

Mitch Gaynor clutched his left arm, blood dripping from his fingers.

And Mayor Ron held a smoking gun.

15

September 20, 1891
Dearest Mary,

    I'm certain you spent the night on your knees for me although you could not yet have received word of my plans. A preacher who has joined the thousands at the border, hoping to make the run for the town of Chandler, held a service.

    We sang many familiar tunes, including my favorite, "Amazing Grace." He preached from Isaiah 43:19. "Behold, I will do a new thing; now it shall spring forth; shall ye not know it? I will even make a way in the wilderness." The words resounded in my heart. The preacher warned against moving ahead of God's timing; God will make everything new and right and beautiful in His time.

    I am torn. My mind was settled, but now I feel ashamed. How can I fail you again? Numbers at the border have swollen beyond count, each one certain that this is his opportunity for a new life. It helps me to pour out my heart to you, even though events will have been decided before you see my words.

    Your loving fiancé,
    Robert Grace

Thursday, September 26

I stood rooted to the spot for the space of a heartbeat. The irony of the situation registered. This was the true reenactment of the original gunfight, in reverse. Dick Gaynor had wounded Bob Grace in the arm; now Bob's grandson Ron had wounded Dick's grandson Mitch the same way. I doubted that it was a fatal wound, but blood dripped in an ominous puddle on the plush beige carpet.

"You'll pay for this." Mitch circled the mayor, an animal made fierce by injury, the difference in their heights menacing under the circumstances. "You shot me on purpose!"

"You stupid—stupid—" The mayor couldn't find a word worthy of the insult that wanted to escape his lips. "Gaynor." A Grace could think of no greater insult. "If I meant to shoot you, I would have done more than nick your arm." Red anger suffused his normally placid face and sent fingers up his bald head. "It was an accident."

"That's one accident too many, if you ask me. First Penn, now me. The Graces have always had a feud with the Gaynors; you can't deny it. You should all be locked up." Mitch shook his fist in the mayor's face, spraying fresh drops of blood on the floor.

"Sit down, both of you." Audie spoke with authority. They complied.

The two men glared at each other, hurling verbal insults, but at least they didn't come to blows. I glanced at the empty gun case and remembered that the mayor still held the gun in his hands. In the high emotions of the moment, he might decide to shoot again. I suppressed a shiver.

I started to reach for the gun then stopped myself. Fingerprints. "Why don't you put the gun on your desk?" I suggested.

Ron jumped, a blank look taking over his face at the interruption. He stared at the gun in his hand as if he had forgotten about it. "Good idea." He hefted the weight in his palm and eyed the mechanism. "I didn't shoot you on purpose, Mitch. I don't even remember pulling the trigger." After brushing aside slivers of glass with a tissue, he set the gun down. He stayed on his feet. He usually did—as short as he was, he looked ridiculous behind the big mayor's desk.

For answer, he received a muttered curse.

"What do you remember?" I asked. "How did the gun case get broken?"

The mayor studied the display case, which held pride of place over his head in the mayoral office. Shards of glass had scattered across the entire end of the office. Cracks marred the frame of his diploma from Grace Gulch High School and his photo with the governor. The only thing untouched was the "Grace World Map," which should please him. Multicolored pushpins still located all the communities and organizations containing the word Grace in their name. The proudest piece of Grace World memorabilia, a Maori tiki from Grace City, New Zealand, had fallen on its side. I closed my eyes, dredging up memories of the office layout from my last visit. What was out of place? I opened them again. I couldn't remember.

"It was the key that broke the case."

Key? It didn't make sense.

"The key to the city." Ron sounded tired. He pointed to the floor.

I walked around to the back of the desk. A three-foot-long copper-plated key marked WELCOME TO GRACE GULCH had fallen to the floor.

"He threatened to throw me out of the town and throw away the key," Mitch said from his spot across the room. "So I said, 'You mean this key?' and I grabbed the thing. We must have knocked into the display case during the tussle." He pointed a finger at the mayor. "That's when he grabbed the gun and shot me."

Blood seeped through a white linen handkerchief tied around Mitch's arms. Audie must have taken care of that.

"If the police don't arrest you, I'll sue."

Ron only shook his head, the anger drained out of him.

Something rumbled in the outer office, and we turned our attention to the door. The EMTs had arrived.

"Who's been shot?" A petite brunette paramedic spoke up, her features suggesting the Fox Indian heritage common in our part of Oklahoma. She spotted the blood on the carpet and looked at Mitch. "Let me see."

Several EMTs trooped in behind her, together with the one officer present. He let the techs do their work. They did the usual things, determining the nature and extent of the wound before they moved the patient. They unwrapped Audie's makeshift bindings as well as cut away the sleeve of Mitch's shirt. Blood soaked the soft cotton. I watched, slightly queasy, unable to look away.

"It looks like this is just a flesh wound, sir. We'll get you to the hospital and have you home in no time." She unfolded a wheelchair.

When she tried to assist Mitch, he shook her off. "My legs are fine." He leaned on the chair with his good arm and pushed up. "You'll be hearing from my lawyer." Mitch sent one last sally to the mayor before he headed out the door. "No Grace is going to get away with it a second time."

"You can get his statement at the hospital," the young tech said to the officer. She directed Mitch through the door before he could renew his complaints.

"No way to keep this quiet." Mayor Ron's face, pale as Swiss cheese, crumpled into worried lines. "I'm sorry to miss your appointment, folks. I always want to talk with the public." He inserted a note of political bonhomie into the words.

Betty the secretary poked her head in the door. "Chief Reiner said he would come as soon as he returns to town. He's out on a 911 call at the old Kirkendall place. It sounds like no one was there."

The officer opened his mouth to speak. The mayor looked at him. "I'll wait for the chief."

The young man hesitated. I felt sorry for him. I could see his police training warring with his respect for the man in charge.

"You may leave." Mayor Ron turned toward us. "Now give me a few moments to speak with these folks."

The officer gulped and left the office.

"It looks like we'll have time for our chat after all. But let's leave this depressing office." Mayor Ron stood up, matching actions to his words. "Betty, see if the cleaning crew can come by early, as soon as the police finish their investigation. Cici, Audie, the conference room?"

We sat at one end of a long, polished maple table. So this is what our tax money went for. I confess the ergonomic chairs cushioned me in comfort. I envisioned the movers and shakers of Grace Gulch crowded into the space during a city council meeting. Betty poured us each a cup of coffee and plopped a box of pastries from Gaynor Goodies in the middle of the table.

Ron spoke in generalities, urging us to try the apple fritters. "They're the best in the county, even if a Gaynor did bake them!" he declared.

I agreed. I ate them at least once a week. "Not today." I smiled. I chose a bran muffin and bit into the thick bread.

Betty departed, leaving the door slightly ajar.

"Now how can I help you folks?" Away from the disaster of his office, the mayor regained his composure. He smiled in cheerful welcome.

I wanted to ask, What were you and Mitch arguing about? My gut told me it had to be about last weekend's events, but a practiced politician like the mayor would sidestep that question. I needed a better opening.

Audie found it for me. "Did either Penn or Mitch

ever discuss the history of Grace Gulch with you? I thought Penn might have interviewed you when he wrote the play."

"Of course. You can't read too much into what happened today. Mitch and I had a friendly bet over your little play. I warned him it was a losing bet; I had history on my side." His grin increased until I was afraid his lips would crack from stretching so far. "He didn't like losing."

"What happened? Exactly?" Since the mayor brought up the subject, I felt I could ask. "When did you grab the gun? Did Mitch threaten you?"

"Why should I answer you?" Ron cleared his throat. "You're not the police."

"But we'll listen with an open mind."

I saw Audie's mouth open to interrupt and frowned him into silence.

"We're not Gaynors or Graces. Neutral, so to speak."

"And you're Cord's friends." A smile twitched at the corners of the mayor's mouth. "To tell the truth, I don't know exactly what happened. Mitch picked up the key and swung it at the gun case. We both went for the gun at the same time—I wanted to prevent a shooting, you understand—and the next thing I knew, the gun had been fired and Mitch was clutching his arm. I don't remember pulling the trigger."

What was he saying? That Mitch shot himself? Why would he do that? Or was this mayor-talk to cover his tracks?

"Were the two of you arguing about the true history

of the land run, Mayor?" Audie leaned forward, elbows folded on the table, calm as a man holding the winning cards.

"What do you mean, the true history of the land run?" Ron's lips snapped into a thin line, and he sank back in his chair. "Everybody knows what happened. You just produced the reenactment."

"Gwen Hardy let us read the Grace letters. The ones Penn used to write the script. We ran across this." Audie reached into his jacket pocket and pulled out the letter we had found.

"It doesn't matter." Ron waved a pudgy hand in the direction of the envelope. "Whatever it says, it's ancient history." His pallor belied his easy denial, and his protest rang hollow.

"If it doesn't matter—then what were the two of you arguing about?" Audie asked.

I held my breath, waiting for his answer.

Pink returned to Ron's cheeks. "Who do you think you are, barging in here and asking me questions?"

He knew more than he was telling. His indignation confirmed our suspicions more strongly than a signed confession would have.

"Tell me what you want, young man, before I have you thrown out on your ear."

Audie remained unruffled. I wondered what went on beneath the surface—was he really calm, or was he acting? He pushed the envelope in Ron's direction with one slender finger. Earnest sincerity marked his face. "Don't you want to know the truth, sir? No matter what you decide to do about it? Before someone else is hurt by this so-called ancient history?"

"Very well." Ron's hand engulfed the envelope and extracted two thin sheets of paper. A faint scent of violets reached my nose.

I could see his lips mouthing the words. "Ready to cheat. . .found a cave. . .ahead of anyone else. . . whatever I must." He looked at the date. "He wrote this on September 19. Three days before the land run. He must have changed his mind." His political mind already put the right spin on the evidence.

The mayor picked up his coffee cup—a tourist cup from Idaho, GRACE CITY painted in black letters on green clay—and paced the conference room. He walked from his seat to the windows that overlooked the gulch, green hills that sloped toward our main street, never far away from the center of town. "He chose well," he murmured. "The story passed down in our family is that he wanted the town to be a place where God's grace would reign. I can't talk about it much publicly, of course—state and religion and all that—but that's what we believe."

" 'He who has been forgiven much loves much,' " Audie quoted. "Even if he was a Sooner, maybe because he was a Sooner, he knew about God's grace firsthand." It was a nice gesture, paying tribute to Grace Gulch's founder without making him a saint. And make no mistake about it, Bob Grace did found the town of Grace Gulch, whether by legal or illegal means.

The mayor faced northwest, to where the Circle G Ranch stood, and didn't say anything for a few minutes. When he resumed his place at the table, both the blustering fighter and the grinning homeboy had disappeared, replaced by a wily politician.

"The ranch belongs to Cord, fair and square. Gaynor didn't go down without a fight. He used every means, legal and illegal, to get my grandfather off his claim."

I thought about that. Ancient history, maybe, but to Cord and any other Grace in town the history was as fresh as this morning's coffee. For starters, Gaynor had tried barn burnings. Tampering with the water supply. Cattle rustling. None of it was proven, but suspicions ran strong.

"Gaynor filed a claim against my grandfather, of course. The courts were overrun with suits about claims for years, but eventually he had his day in court. You can check at the courthouse in Chandler for a record of the trial. All it amounted to was a lot of finger-pointing and name-calling. Gaynor didn't have a lick of proof." The mayor wagged his finger at Audie. "And see here, young man, that trial was over a century ago. Nothing can change the court's decision. The land belongs to the Grace family, fair and square."

"Of course it does. No one is questioning that." Audie tapped the letter with his fingers. "But that's not the problem. Did Penn Hardy come to you about this letter from Bob Grace?"

"Maybe he did. Maybe he didn't." The mayor had regained his balance. "It doesn't matter."

"But it does." I put in my two cents' worth. "Grace Gulch history is like a sacred text to anyone with the Grace name. No one wants to find out that Bob Grace was a cheat and a scallywag."

"And this letter"—again, Audie tapped the thin papers—"proves that at the very least, he considered cheating. And once the idea took hold in his mind, he may have given in. Dorian Gray warns us, 'The only way to get rid of temptation is to yield to it.' "

"Go peddle your insults elsewhere." The mayor's lips twisted in a snarl.

I glanced around the room, seeking something, anything, to divert their attention away from confrontation. A cartoon on the wall caught my eye. Three longhorn cattle lay on the ground. The long ears of one bent over his eyes; the second, over his ears; and the third, over his mouth. In the distance, a rustler took off with the rest of the herd, a cowboy version of "hear no evil." What the mayor didn't know could not hurt him.

Or maybe he did know and made a pretense of ignorance. The mayor took great pride in his name. He was a Grace, and nobody could take that from him.

But what if someone threatened to drag the Grace name through the mud?

Would that be enough to kill for?

Reiner arrived with Frances Waller, their boots splattered with mud, and Frances looked wet and miserable. The bogus 911 tip had resulted in nothing more than a cold drenching.

"What's this I hear about you shooting Mitch?" Reiner asked in his most belligerent tone.

I clenched my teeth. I decided to stay put as long as they let me. The mayor hadn't convinced me of his innocence, but neither did I believe he planned to shoot Mitch. Reiner sounded ready to convict him without a trial.

"I'm not saying anything to you without my lawyer."

Reiner sighed and turned his attention to Audie and me. "What are you two doing here this morning? You'd better not interfere with an official police investigation."

"Now, Reiner, they just had an appointment to see me this morning. Let them go." It was nice of the mayor to speak up for us, but I couldn't help wondering if he wanted to keep the police from learning about our conversation.

Or the letter. As far as I was concerned, the police didn't need to know about it. I could see the envelope on the table, close to the mayor's right hand. If I reached for it, would Reiner notice and insist on seeing it?

"We had some questions about the festival, and the mayor was kind enough to give us a few minutes of his time after Mr. Gaynor left for the hospital." Audie leaned against the table, his hand resting ever so gently on the letter, a perfectly natural pose. "We'll take our leave now that you are here." He straightened, tucking the letter into his hand and slipping it into his coat pocket.

"Wait a minute," Reiner said. "Did you witness the shooting?"

"No." Both Audie and I spoke at the same time.

"Someone called 911." Frances spoke up for the first time.

"We heard. . .noises. . .coming from the mayor's office. And we heard a shot." I leveled an apologetic look at the mayor. "So Betty called."

"When we opened the door, Mr. Gaynor was holding his arm and he was bleeding," Audie offered.

"We'll need your statements. You two and that secretary, Betty. Officer Waller?"

"Follow me, please," she said. The dry heat flowing from ceiling vents had dried out Frances's uniform. Once again she looked calm and in charge.

We followed her out the door. And left Mayor Ron in the clutches of a police officer who would like to arrest him for murder.

September 21, 1891 Excerpt A
Dearest Mary,
After posting my last letter, I decided that I must go to the cave I found. While the marshals were occupied with quieting a riotous drinking crowd, and while Gaynor spoke at length with the preacher, I slipped out of the camp and rode fast for the cave.

I struggled all night. During the fading daylight, I bettered the concealment to the entrance and hid Patches behind the brush. Then I backed myself into a narrow fissure in the rocks, barely big enough for a man to sit. I cleared my mind as I often do on a cattle drive, emptying my mind of everything except danger signs.

I was as twitchy as a greenhorn. Every time a coyote howled, I jumped as though hearing the preacher's words of warning. Every time a cloud passed in front of the moon, I felt cut off from God's light.

Thursday, September 26

"That's the second time the police have needed statements from us within the past week." Audie guided me by my arm out to my car, dulled by the morning's drizzle to olive green. At least the trench coat I had chosen to wear kept me dry from shoulders to toe, and I had a rain hood to minimize damage to my hair.

"And I hope we don't have to do it again for a long time." I blamed the shiver that passed through me on the cool weather, not on the scene we had just witnessed.

"Everything will be okay," Audie said, his voice as warm as a pleasant spring breeze, and some of the chill lifted.

Still, I was glad to get into the car and turn on the heater. The defroster on the back window of my car made driving on mornings like this a little easier. I waited without speaking until the air turned hot and steamy and a delightful warm stupor enveloped me. If only I could ease the shivering in my mind by such a simple method. I started the windshield wipers and backed out of the parking space.

"Nothing like a bout of fisticuffs to start my morning off right." Audie spoke in a lighthearted tone. "If I want to escape violence, maybe I should move back to Chicago. After all, Solomon warns us, 'My son, do not go along with them. . . . For their feet rush into sin, they are swift to shed blood.' "

Move back to Chicago? The warmth fled in an instant.

Audie must have sensed my distress. He turned his cobalt blue eyes on me. "I hope you know I'm kidding. Are you doing okay?"

"I'm more confused than ever. What do you think

happened? Was it really an accident?" That's the finding I wanted: an unintentional accident that no one could be blamed for. Except, of course, for people who thought any gun threatened humanity and therefore blamed the mayor for keeping weapons in his office. The antigun lobby had few proponents in Grace Gulch.

"Or did the mayor shoot Gaynor on purpose? Or"—he hurried on before I could protest—"did Gaynor somehow shoot himself?" He shook his head. "That doesn't seem possible."

I stopped by Gaynor's Goodies and picked up a dozen cinnamon pecan muffins and another half dozen apple raisin, then parked behind my store as usual. The minute hand landed straight up on the ten o'clock hour when I opened for business. No customers arrived while I readied my cash drawer and brewed a pot of coffee. Audie grabbed one of the muffins and settled into a folding chair by the changing rooms. Did he intend to stay all day? That might be nice. Pressing his fingers into the napkin, he ate the last of the crumbs, then threw away the remains and washed his hands.

"Maybe if we act it out, we can figure out what happened. Like we did at the Gulch."

"Good idea." I poured myself a cup of coffee. My hand slipped and a bit spilled onto the carpet. Fortunately, the dark beige absorbed spills without ruining the color. I bent over to do a quick wipe-up job and made a mental note to get the carpets cleaned next month, before the Christmas shopping season started.

"Let me do that." Audie knelt on the floor. "No

need to muss up that pretty outfit and get those bell-bottoms dirty. I can scrub carpets with the best of them." He knelt a moment longer than necessary, staring at the floor. I wondered if he was thinking about the other carpet stains we had seen that morning, as I was. He looked up at me and smiled.

"As far as I can see, there are only three possibilities about what happened this morning." He stood and brushed off the cuffs of his pants. "Accident. Or the mayor shot Gaynor on purpose. Or Gaynor shot himself. Which is the most likely?"

"Accident," I answered without hesitation.

"Perhaps. But let's act it out anyhow. Your stapler can be the gun. I'll be Gaynor; you be Grace." His face transformed into an angry mask. "You mean this key?" He knocked a pen against the counter, scattering papers like the broken glass must have rained on the floor.

What did the mayor say happened next? He reached for the gun to prevent an accident. I grabbed the stapler. Audie's hands came down on top of mine. The pressure released a staple.

"That was an accident," I said.

"Let's try it again," Audie suggested. He reached for the stapler without warning and pointed it toward his left forearm before my hands made contact.

"Suggestive," Audie murmured. "Even if the mayor's finger pulled the trigger—"

"Mitch could have directed the gun at himself. But why would he do that?" We looked at each other. "And does this have anything to do with Penn's murder?"

"We know the mayor had a motive. A couple of motives."

I shook my head a single time.

"Yes, he did," Audie insisted. "I agree that the issue about the last election seems a trifle slim. But preserving the Grace family honor—the mayor takes that very seriously."

"But if we're suspecting the mayor of the murder, why would Mitch shoot himself?"

"Can you help me?" A soft voice interrupted our conversation. Absorbed by our discussion, I hadn't heard the customer enter. How much had the lady overheard? My ears burned.

"Why don't we sleep on it and discuss it in the morning," Audie said. "Good day, Mrs. Beresford." With a nod, he left my store.

I turned my attention to my customer. Patti Beresford was a sweet, grandmotherly type, hard of hearing but sharp as a tack. She glanced at the stapler still in my hands but didn't ask. She wouldn't spread gossip, either, a rarity in the town's rumor mill.

"My granddaughter is getting married in December," she said.

"Congratulations!" I scrambled through my mental files. I had met the young woman when Patti brought her to church events over the years. "That must be Terry. Who is the lucky man?"

"An accountant, over Arcadia way."

I drove to Arcadia, home of a round barn and Hillbillies, a fun little café on Old Route 66, fairly often.

"So how can I help you today?"

She plunged into a description of Terry's plan for a costume wedding and her need for an outfit. "Something from the '50s, but not too expensive, dear." We made arrangements for Terry to come in with her grandmother and discuss her plans.

The remainder of the morning passed quickly. I was ready to close the store for lunch when the doorbell jangled. For a second time, I set aside the tuna salad sandwich I had brought from home. Would this be one of those days when I could only eat in small bites?

Suzanne peeked out from beneath an umbrella. Her face looked pinched, her hair, flat. Not a good day.

Oh, no, I never mended her dress. She needed to return it to Audie, and he would understand the delay. Still, it wasn't smart business to forget a client. I swallowed my bite of salad and brushed a napkin across my mouth.

"Don't let me interrupt your lunch." Suzanne started to back out the door.

"I'm fine." I rewrapped my sandwich and stood up. "How can I help you today? I'm afraid that I haven't finished the repairs to your dress yet."

"Oh, that." She waved ringed fingers in dismissal. "I'm not worried about that. In fact, I'm not here about business at all. I wanted to talk, that's all. Or should I come back another time?"

"Now is fine." My heart skipped a beat. I turned my store sign to CLOSED. "Do you mind if I finish eating while we talk?"

Suzanne shook her head.

"Would you like some coffee? A muffin?" I handed her the open box of muffins.

"I'll take a cup of coffee. Black." She reached for a muffin. That was a surprise. I had never seen Suzanne eat anything at rehearsal or elsewhere. She took as good care of her figure as a Hollywood starlet.

I poured her coffee in a disposable cup. She picked pecans off the top of her muffin and chewed each one. She broke off tiny pieces of bread and ate them with evident pleasure.

I finished my sandwich, watching Suzanne carefully. Something was wrong with my guest. On Monday, when we first learned about her affair with Penn, she had been upset. Time had not improved her spirits. If anything, she seemed worse.

Suzanne set aside the bottom half of her muffin. "I heard about what happened at the mayor's office this morning."

That didn't surprise me. There might be a few people left in Lincoln County who hadn't heard about the shooting, but I doubted it. But why did that bring her to my store this afternoon?

"You were there?" A slight rise in her voice made it a question.

"In the outer office, yes. We didn't actually witness. . .anything."

"So you don't know what they were arguing about?"

I shook my head.

"I was hoping you could tell me what made them

angry enough to start shooting."

My hackles rose in defense of the mayor. "We don't know what happened. It sounds like it was an accident."

She dismissed that with another wave of red fingernails. "There was an argument. A gun was fired. I don't care who shot whom." In spite of the casual words, her face betrayed the gravity of her emotions. "That could have been me with the gun. I don't mean that I had a disagreement with either the mayor or Mr. Gaynor. I mean. . ." She buried her nose in her cup of coffee, as if gathering courage to continue. "I mean with Penn. I was so angry that if I'd had a gun, I would have shot him."

I sat back in my chair. Was I listening to a murder confession? Why had I locked the door? Could I reach my phone and dial 911?

Suzanne's hand trembled and she dropped the cup, coffee spreading in a small black puddle in the same spot as my previous spill. At least the plastic cup couldn't shatter.

"I'm so sorry." She fell to her knees and began sopping up the liquid with a napkin. I considered taking advantage of the distraction to call the police, but I didn't think she was dangerous. I grabbed a towel and bent next to her. Warm liquid splashed on my hand. Tears.

My last doubts fled. This woman could not have committed murder. Her heart was broken. I helped her back into her chair and handed her a box of tissues.

"I'm a mess." She sniffed. "I've been thinking about

it all week. First, I let myself get involved with a married man. When he refused to leave his family for me and tried to end things, I was so angry. I hated him."

What did people say? The opposite of love wasn't hate; it was indifference. She wouldn't have hated Penn if she hadn't loved him.

She cried, but it was different than her tears on Monday. In retrospect, that day seemed more like a stage performance of grief. Today, sobs like a child's racked her body, heartbroken gulps. When she spoke, I couldn't understand her words. "Shh." I patted her back. I didn't know what else to do for a woman in turmoil, unless it was my little sister. "Go ahead and cry it out."

It felt like an hour before Suzanne's sobs slowed down, but in reality the clock indicated only five minutes had passed. She used half the box of tissues to blow her nose and wipe the tears from her face.

"I feel so dirty and guilty. I didn't pull the trigger on Penn, but I was so mad that I could have. You must hate me. I know I hate myself."

I thought back to my judgmental attitude on Monday. No wonder she thought I hated her. Of course she turned to Audie for comfort. How little like Jesus I had acted. I felt a degree of the shame I saw etched on Suzanne's face. Thank God that He had given me a second chance to help. This time, I would try to make a difference.

"Oh, Suzanne." I sighed. "I'm ashamed of myself. I was so busy blaming you that I didn't stop to think how you must feel."

She smiled weakly, tears dimming the deep sea green of her eyes. "You had every right."

Lord, help me. I sent up a prayer and opened my mouth to explain. "Yes, what you did was wrong. Sin, to use that old-fashioned word. But we all sin, every day. And God loves us anyway, and He wants His children to love others the way He loves us. That's why I'm ashamed of myself. I judged you instead of showing you God's love."

"I don't deserve God's love. You don't know everything I've done."

"I don't deserve God's love either. Nobody does. The Bible says that we are separated from God—His enemies. But even though we are God's enemies, He sent His Son Jesus to die for us. I can't imagine that. But God—God sent His Son to take my place. Jesus took the punishment that I deserved. He loves me that much. And He loves you that much." I took Suzanne's trembling fingers between my own. "He's wrapped up that love like a birthday present, in His Son Jesus. All you have to do is accept His gift."

"I'd like to think that's possible." Suzanne wiped another tissue across her face. The pain lines around her mouth had eased a little. She stood up to leave. I could only pray that the words I'd shared would take root. She tucked into the restroom and emerged a few minutes later with her makeup retouched.

"Thank you for taking the time to talk with me today." A degree of assurance had returned to her voice.

"Any time." We hugged and said good-bye. God had presented me with an unlikely new friendship. "I'll have your dress ready by Saturday, for sure."

A few minutes later, I opened the store for the afternoon. My attitude had changed. I found myself praying for Suzanne, that she would understand that God loved her. I prayed for Mitch Gaynor, that his wound would not be serious. I spoke with God about everyone involved in the investigation, for both my sisters, without a trace of jealousy for once, for every customer who came into the shop. The hours sped by, fast-forwarded by prayer. The worries about the murder, and what to do about it, dropped away in my own personal praise concert.

My good mood lasted into the evening. I browned a chicken breast in butter, flavored with a mixture of paprika and cumin, and steamed fresh asparagus spears—an indulgence I allowed myself at the grocery store. I should call Cord. He must have heard about what happened at the city offices by now.

He picked up the phone on the third ring. "What's up?"

I explained what we had seen and heard and surmised—everything except the fact that the mayor was still a solid suspect in Penn's death. "It looks like Mitch might have aimed the gun at himself."

"I suppose that city slicker came up with that harebrained idea."

"Would you rather think that your cousin shot Mitch on purpose?" Cord was my friend, but sometimes he was so thickheaded.

"Of course not." Cord drew in a deep breath. "Thanks for filling in the details." He asked me what I wanted to do on the weekend. He agreed to escort me to a couple of estate sales.

I felt so good that I even decided to enter my store accounts on my computer. While online, I checked the status of the stock market. Something about stocks niggled at my mind. Something Dina had said. What was it? *I wonder if someone is cooking the books.* Dina had said the *Sequoian* might be in financial trouble.

The paper was a publicly traded company. I remembered when Mitch first put it on the market and published daily updates as the shares rose in value. In fact, that's what started my interest in the stock market. I tracked the price for an economics class in high school. I hadn't checked its stock value for a long time, though.

I confirmed the paper's symbol, SEQ, on their Web site and checked the NASDAQ listings. The price had spiked recently. I frowned. That didn't seem possible. I browsed through the history of the stock and discovered that the price had started a steady increase about six months ago. What had triggered the upward trend?

Further investigation revealed that there had been a lot of movement in the stock, pushing the price up. Mitch Gaynor held on to a slim majority of 51 percent. Was any one party behind the purchase of falling stock? As in a hostile takeover?

Time sped by while I chased the elusive stock. One site led to another until the minute hand on my office clock ticked past midnight. At last I tracked down the person behind the takeover attempt.

Penn Hardy.

Mitch Gaynor had a whopper of a motive to stop his rival in his tracks.

17

September 21, 1891 Excerpt B

I was foolish to think I could find peace apart from God. I confessed my sinful thoughts of cheating and stealing to make my dream come true. After that, sleep came easily.

I had the strangest dream. You and I founded a town on land including the very cave where I slept. It was a place where God's grace reigned. When bad times came—I saw some awful droughts in years ahead, ground so dry that the wind carried the very dust in the air—we survived and overcame.

I awoke refreshed before dawn, moved aside the bushes, and rode Patches back to the waiting crowds at the border. This may not be our time—although I pray that it is—but I trust God to fulfill His word.

Your loving fiancé,
Robert Grace

Friday, September 27

I retired to bed about one in the morning but couldn't fall asleep. Suzanne, Gwen, Ron, Mitch.

Their four names repeated in my head like a murderous refrain. Each of them had motive and opportunity to kill Penn Hardy. Who wanted his death badly enough to kill him? *God, You're going to have to show me what happened.* With that simple prayer, I nodded off and slept soundly until the alarm buzzed at half past seven.

I chose my simplest outfit for Friday—western jeans, silver buckle, hair in a no-nonsense braid down my back, and a red plaid blouse with a silver button on the breast pocket—grabbed a ready-to-go box of donuts from the grocery store and made it to the store by nine with a minute to spare.

Had only a week passed since the Race for Grace Gulch reenactment kicked off this year's Land Run Days? The past weekend seemed as much a part of ancient history as the original feud, not a mere seven days.

One glazed donut and a cup of hazelnut coffee later, I felt ready to greet my first customers. The goods I had gathered for sales during Land Run Days were depleted; the time for a clearance sale had arrived. It would encourage people to buy less popular items. I looked through my wares and decided on rock-bottom prices. Some people tried to barter me down to a giveaway price. I refused to do that. What didn't sell today would sell eventually. Everything old is new again; styles cycled through fashions like the earth rotated on its axis.

That kept me busy until noon. I found a few minutes to complete the repair of Suzanne's dress and wrapped it up for her. The bell rang, and Dina and

Audie entered. Dina danced, excitement popping from her pores. Or maybe it was the red dye she used to touch up her hair since I saw her last.

"I hope you're hungry for a ham salad croissant." Audie held up a bag from Gaynor Goodies. I had to smile at him, at his thoughtfulness.

"Wait till you hear what we've been doing." Dina took a huge bite of croissant and swallowed it, closing her eyes in appreciation. "We've been down at the MGM."

Since the theater was Audie's workplace and Dina volunteered there, I wondered why she thought that would surprise me. "And?"

"We wanted to see if we could figure out who had access to the guns in the prop box. Who could have taken the third gun, the one that's missing?"

"A lot of people did." How does this help the investigation?

"Don't you want to know what we found out?" my smart-alecky sister fussed at me.

"Okay, what? Anyone from our list of suspects?"

"Suzanne"—when Dina turned eighteen, she decided she could drop the childhood formality of calling all adults Miss or Mister—"had access, of course, since she's in the theater troupe."

"But she's often said she dislikes handling weapons."

"Don't argue." Audie wagged a finger at me when I started to protest. "She mentioned it when she joined the theater. She said she hoped she never had to play a cop or a murderer because she doesn't like even touching the things."

I didn't bother to suggest the idea of misdirection. I agreed that it didn't seem likely. After our talk yesterday, I knew her anger at Penn only came to a boil in the last month. "Let's stick to the facts. We're looking for the big three, right? Means, motive, opportunity? And the ones who had the best opportunity were the mayor, Mitch, Penn's widow, and Suzanne."

"If we're being totally honest, we probably should include Cord," Audie said.

"Audie's right." Dina grinned at me. "Close your mouth. Or else a fly might go in. Cord did have opportunity, although we know he didn't do it."

I gritted my teeth. "All right. We'll add Cord to the list."

"Suzanne has all three." Audie spoke the words calmly enough. "Besides opportunity, we know she had a motive. She was having an affair with Penn, but he wanted to break it off. And Dina already knows about that, so I'm not spreading gossip. Number two, the means. She had access to the gun. . .if she knows how to work the thing."

"So Suzanne stays on the list." Dina whipped out a steno book and pencil; she looked like a regular cub reporter. "How about the mayor? The guns belonged to him. He might have another Colt in his collection."

My memory flashed to the gun case in his office. I didn't get a close enough look at the gun used in yesterday's shooting to identify it as the same model.

"And he certainly knows how to shoot," Dina said. "What Oklahoma boy doesn't? But he doesn't have a motive, does he?"

Audie and I looked at each other. We hadn't told Dina about the letter we had found. I thought about the three days between the last letter and the land run and wondered if Grace had changed his mind. We still might not know the whole story.

"Penn opposed his reelection," I reminded her. "And we think Penn might have uncovered some skeletons in the Grace family tree that the mayor wanted to keep quiet."

"Okay." She dragged out the last syllable. "He stays on the list. Gwen is next. I suppose her motive would be Penn's affair with Suzanne."

"But she never came to the theater," Audie said. "I think it's safe to cross her off the list."

"Unless she had the same model gun. But that seems unlikely. She might have a modern weapon, but not a historical piece like that."

"I wish we knew if the police had found the murder weapon," Audie said. "I haven't seen anything in the paper since they revealed it was a model 1892."

"Of course Cord had access to the guns," Dina said and grinned. "So he had means and opportunity. But he had no motive. We can leave him off the list."

"He had a motive." I didn't look at Audie while the words dragged out of me. He was right. We had to do this the proper way and look at everyone. "Penn threatened to publish a rumor about mad cow disease in Cord's herd."

Dina's mouth dropped open. "No way."

"It's not true, but just the rumor could shut down Cord's business and do permanent harm."

"But we have his testimony that he felt the bullet fly by his arm." Now Audie was the one bending over backwards to play fair. "And you put blanks in the guns. I don't think it was Cord."

"What about my boss?" Dina tapped the pencil against her teeth. "He might have had means. He interviewed you about the reenactment, didn't he? Did you show him the guns?"

"I showed him the guns and explained that the mayor had lent them to us for the duration of the celebration. I thought a little back-scratching wouldn't hurt, but now I wish I'd kept my mouth shut. But we don't know of any motive Mitch had for wanting Penn dead."

The bite of croissant turned to dry toast in my mouth, the mayonnaise lingering in my throat like acid. "He had a motive."

Two heads—one blond, one Christmas red—swiveled in my direction. "What's that?" Audie sounded upset, as if I had been keeping a secret from him.

"I discovered it last night. Dina told me that the *Sequoian* might be in financial trouble, and I decided to check it out."

"What did you learn?"

"Penn was behind a takeover bid. He's been buying every available share." Another piece of information fell into place. "And Suzanne told us that Mitch carried on about needing money for some business deal." I looked at my sister. "And the fuss about the number of newspapers you printed. I think he printed fewer copies than they used to, to save money. He was pinching pennies, trying to save his business. His family's business, going back to the Grace-Gaynor feud."

"Phew." Audie intertwined his long fingers. "What is it they say about motives for murder? There's only a handful—revenge, jealousy, money."

"I thought it was *cui bono*—who benefits?" Dina tossed her head. "I guess it's another way of saying the same thing."

"Let me see that list." I took the steno book from Dina's hands. "We've tentatively eliminated the widow. And Cord." I smiled at Audie. "Have we established that Mitch had the means? Did you leave him alone with the guns at any point? He couldn't have taken one with you looking on."

Audie shook his head, frustration evident in the movement. "I did. On the morning of the play, he came into the theater. He asked if he could borrow a phone to make a call, because he had forgotten his cell phone. I was busy taking care of last-minute details, so I left him alone in my office."

"Suzanne. Mayor Ron. Gaynor." My heart twisted. I still didn't want the murderer to be someone I knew. I looked at the package that held the dress I had mended for Suzanne and remembered our last conversation.

"I don't think Suzanne did it." I shared the conversation I had with her. "At first I thought she was confessing to a murder. I was pretty scared for a few minutes! Then I realized that she was talking about her affair with Penn. I know she's an actress, but her remorse rang true."

"Let's think on it," Audie said. "Cici, are you still up for dinner tonight?"

Dina looked at the two of us. "I can tell when I'm not wanted." She pretended to huff but couldn't hold back the grin from her face. "Don't worry, I won't spill the beans. I've got to get to class." She blew us a kiss on her way out the door.

Audie arched a pale eyebrow over his darkened eyes.

"She misunderstood the invitation." The words stumbled on their way out of my mouth. "We've been working on this investigation together, that's all."

"No, she didn't." Audie's blue eyes bore into me like a laser light, exposing my deepest feelings. "I like your little sister—or should I call her your niece?—but I want some time alone with you."

"Oh." I didn't know what else to say. "Yes, I accept. Shall we plan on the Buffalo Herd or the Gulch?"

"The Buffalo Herd. I'm ready for Old Jim to buffalo me into his choice of dinner." Audie grinned. The owner, Old Jim Wiseman, never used a menu and only served the special of the day—always something made from buffalo meat. Audie tipped my head to meet his dazzling eyes. "When this is over, you and I need to have a talk."

I warmed from head to foot, followed by a delightful chill. "Okay," I said in a small voice.

He brushed his lips across mine, wrapping me in warmth once again. "I'll pick you up here when you close up shop."

The phone rang as Audie pulled up on the street. It was Gwen Hardy.

"Cici. I'm glad I caught you." She sounded more composed than she had on Monday.

"I found more of the Grace letters. Are you interested? I don't want them around."

More letters? Something that would reveal what did happen on the day of the land run? I couldn't wait. "Absolutely. We'll be by in a few minutes."

I grabbed a waterproof plastic bag and put on a fringed buckskin jacket—one of the advantages of western wear—before meeting Audie outside. He stood on the sidewalk, holding the door of his Focus open for my convenience. My hero.

"Gwen Hardy found more of Bob Grace's letters!" I was grinning so widely that it hurt. "I told her we'd be right over." We stopped by the widow's house and then drove to the Buffalo Herd.

When Old Jim described the day's special, Audie and I nodded agreement. His granddaughter Sara waited on us, bringing out heaping bowls of salad. I dug in with relish.

"I have an idea about our investigation," Audie said. "In the best theatrical tradition, we should do an encore performance of the gunfight."

My mouth dropped open. I shut it and swallowed the lettuce, dabbing at the dressing that dribbled from the corner of my mouth. "Why?"

"Maybe we can jar one of our suspects into confessing." He wiggled his eyebrows. "Isn't that what always happens when Poirot gathers his suspects?"

"This is rural Oklahoma, not England."

"Same principle." Audie waved his hand, rejecting my objection. Sara appeared in response to his gesture. She refilled our coffee cups and left, standing at a discreet distance.

Audie lowered his voice. "We have two primary suspects, right?"

I leaned forward to hear. Out of the corner of my eye I saw Sara smiling. *Great, by tomorrow the whole town will be abuzz with news of a romantic dinner between the two of us. On top of the milkshake we shared the other day, they'll be asking for the wedding date. And what we're really doing is trying to solve a murder.* Speaking of which. . . "The mayor and Mitch Gaynor," I agreed.

"They both probably think they're in the clear. Above suspicion, and all that."

"Reiner wouldn't cover up a murder."

Audie placed a finger on my lips to remind me to lower my voice. The contact burned where it touched my flesh. I glanced in Sara's direction. Perfect! She caught that, too.

"No, but he might not look in the right direction. I figure we can nudge him along. Here's my idea. Gather everybody who was in the play, and everybody who was in the crowd in front of the saloon, together. Everyone who is still in town, that is."

"What will be our excuse for getting them back there?" I balked at the thought of asking people to return to the site of bad memories. Okay, they had probably all been back downtown since last Saturday, but not for the express purpose of reliving those horrific minutes. "I wish the police could invite them."

"It shouldn't be too hard." Audie grinned. "Appeal to their vanity. Get new actors for the drama. Ask the mayor and Mitch to play the roles as prominent scions of their respective clans. Explain that we want to see if Penn missed anything in his version of the land run."

I mulled over the idea. It had possibilities. The mayor would love a chance to play the ham. If he was innocent. And if he was guilty? Well then, maybe he would want to use the play as a smokescreen to throw suspicion on someone else.

"We need the others there as camouflage," Audie said. "So they don't suspect a setup."

Ever since Sara poured the last cup of coffee, Audie had held onto my hands. He bent his head and whispered so that only I could hear. The closest customers sat across the room; no one could hear. I wished he was whispering romantic words instead of investigative secrets.

"That gives us until noon tomorrow to set everything up. Do you think we can do it?"

"All the better. They won't have time to reconsider and back out." Audie raised one of my hands to his lips. His warm breath played across my knuckles like a spring breeze. "Why don't we each call half the people on the list?

"Uh, sure." With his hand cradling my now forest fire hot fingers, I would have agreed to anything.

"Good. It's decided then." With a wicked smile,

Audie signaled for Sara. "We'll share a turtle cheesecake for dessert."

I started to protest, but Audie insisted. "Fine, then. Let's look at the rest of Grace's letters while we wait for dessert."

Sara refilled our coffee cups and brought out a piece of cheesecake and two forks. We ignored them while we read through the letters that reflected Bob Grace's heart and his love for his Mary. How I wanted to be loved like that. I looked at the man sitting across from me. Was it possible? Was this the man God had for me? Maybe. I smiled.

Audie caught the smile. "Find something interesting?"

I blushed. "I was just thinking how much Bob Grace loved his wife. And how much she must have loved him."

"Ah, yes. Lucky man. Maybe Wilde had it right again. 'Women love us for our defects. If we have enough of them, they will forgive us everything.' "

Then you wouldn't be very lovable, because I can't see many defects. I hid my hot face behind the next envelope. The words swam in front of my eyes then gradually cleared. "I lined up with thousands," the letter stated.

"Audie." My voice sounded strangled to my ears. "I know who the murderer must be."

18

September 22, 1891

Dearest Mary,

I am here on our land! God is faithful!

This morning I lined up with thousands at the border to the unassigned lands. The bugle sounded at the stroke of noon. Patches flattened his neck and began a flat-out run, seeking the front of the herd.

We soon left the other settlers behind. I did not see anyone for long minutes, until at last I caught sight of Gaynor's black horse as I neared the cave where I kept vigil on Sunday night. We crested the final hill, neck and neck. I was sure that Gaynor's big horse would have the advantage.

Then the miracle happened. Gaynor's horse stumbled over a rock. A small thing, for it only slowed him down; but Patches made his way down the hill like the sure-footed cow pony he is.

I passed the flag stake and grabbed it. "This claim belongs to Bob Grace!" I shouted. That nettled Gaynor. I had to urge him to continue to the far side of the river, or he would have missed out on a claim altogether.

God be praised, our dream has begun!

Your loving fiancé,

Robert Grace

Friday, September 27

Audie's head snapped up. "What have you found?" He glanced around, making sure our waitress was out of earshot. The other customers had paid their check and left.

"Or at least I know who it isn't." I handed over the letters I had been reading, dated immediately before and after the land run. "God convicted Grace that what he planned to do was wrong. He ran the race fair and square." I managed a slight chuckle. "Cord should be pleased. So should the mayor."

"So Penn wrote the true story after all," Audie mused, his fingers tapping on the table. "That means the mayor had no motive—that we know of—to kill Penn. And that means—"

"Mitch is probably our man." We looked at each other for a long moment, my heart pounding hard in my chest. I lost all interest in the cheesecake still waiting between us.

"Careful." Audie tucked the letter away and put them all back in the plastic bag. "I think we should still ask both men to take part in the reenactment tomorrow. And it's time to tell the police what we've learned. They need to keep an eye on Mitch. And to convince him that he needs to come, if he objects."

"At least the exercise should demonstrate that Mitch—or whoever takes his place in the crowd—could have fired unnoticed because everyone was watching the gunfight."

A big grin broke across Audie's face. "And I know

just how to do it." He told me what he had in mind. I agreed that it sounded like a good plan.

We asked for a box for the cheesecake, eager as we were to leave and set up things for tomorrow before much more time passed. We decided to talk to the police last. If we told them first, they might try to stop us. Audie dropped me off and went home to make his share of the calls. I stayed on the phone until half past ten. Audie called a few minutes later. Everyone on the list had agreed to come to the Gulch at noon on Saturday.

"Did you have any trouble convincing Mitch?" I asked.

"No. He said it sounded like a good idea, and he's bringing a photographer along to take pictures. I wonder if he expects to change history this time."

We had greater concerns than changing Grace Gulch history, and that is why we met on Frances Waller's doorstep shortly after seven on Saturday morning. It was time to enlist the help of the police, and I had to get to the store by nine. Even a murder investigation couldn't close down business.

Of course there was a chance Frances would be working, but I relaxed when I spotted her indigo blue coupe in the parking lot in front of her apartment. She opened her door a crack, almost unrecognizable beneath some kind of facial goop, her hair wrapped in a towel, and dressed in jeans and college T-shirt. "Cici. Audie. Give me a minute." She shut the door in our faces. We waited five long minutes in the cool morning air, listening to the calls of the siskins, wondering if we had made the right move. She reappeared, face clean, hair combed down around her shoulders. "Come in."

Catching her dressed like an ordinary civilian made it easier to tell her what was on our minds.

"We wanted to talk to you. . .about Penn's death."

Her shoulders straightened. "You know I can't do that. It's an ongoing investigation." Even without her uniform, she projected a police presence.

I looked at Audie. He shrugged, as if to say, It's up to you.

"We were concerned when Dina and Cord were involved with the investigation." I didn't want to put her on the defensive by saying what I really felt. *How could you suspect my sister?* "So we decided to ask around on our own."

Frances raised an eyebrow at that. "Why don't you sit down while I make some coffee? It sounds like this may take awhile."

We waited another few minutes. I looked through a stack of books on her end table, surprised to find a few Christian romances tucked in among police manuals. Well, well, was she a romantic at heart? My watch read half-past seven when she returned with four cups in hand, two from the Grace Gulch Police Department and the others, buffalo-shaped mugs dated with Oklahoma's recent centennial.

"I called the chief to come over," she said without preamble. "He needs to hear whatever you have to say, as well."

Ah, well. So much for gaining her sympathetic ear. We sipped the coffee—hot, strong, perfect for a wake-up cup—until we heard the crunch of car tires on gravel. Our hostess opened the door for Reiner before he could knock and then handed him a cup of coffee.

"What's this I hear about the two of you interfering with our investigation?" He stomped over and sat down in Frances's recliner without spilling a drop.

Interfering? No one we had spoken with seemed upset with our visits. Unless the mayor complained to Reiner during their interview.

"I read your statements about the accident in the mayor's office."

Of course. "So you have ruled it as an accidental shooting?"

"For now. Although two accidents in one week is too much of a coincidence. You two were at the scene of the crime both times. Another coincidence?"

I couldn't argue with that.

"But Penn's death was no accident." Audie made it a statement.

"Do you have any forensics reports back yet? Have they found the gun?" I asked.

Reiner and Frances looked at each other, silently agreeing not to share that information.

"It wasn't the gun Cord used, was it?"

Frances blinked at my question, but I decided that I didn't need an answer to continue. "Cord helped us figure out the angle of the shot. It had to come from the direction of the Gulch. And these were the people who were standing there." I showed them our well-worn list of suspects.

Again Reiner and Frances exchanged looks. "Tell us what you think you know," Reiner said. I suppose he couldn't help the sneer that crept into his voice.

I brought out the steno book Dina had used to list the big three—means, motive, opportunity—and explained everything we had learned. Frances made notes. It took forty-five minutes to finish.

"Is that it?" Reiner sat up in the recliner. "Is that why you dragged me away from home on my day off? You know, you really should leave the questioning to the police."

I looked to Frances. "We'll look into what you have told us," she said.

"That's not all," Audie said. "We've arranged for everyone involved to come back to town at noon today. We're going to put on an encore performance, with Mitch and the mayor playing the major roles this time."

"And we could use your help." Actually, I thought they could use our help. After all, hadn't we pretty much uncovered the murderer for them? If today went as we hoped, all that remained for the police was to clamp handcuffs on the murderer's wrists.

"I can come." Frances spoke up before Reiner could forbid it. "What do you need me to do?"

Reiner wouldn't let himself be outdone by a subordinate. "I'll be there. I don't know what fool plan you've concocted, but I don't want anybody hurt this time."

We explained the roles we wanted both of them to play, and they agreed. Ten minutes to nine. Enough time to snag a box of donuts from Gaynor Goodies before I opened for business.

Ordinarily I enjoy Saturday mornings at the store.

More children come in on Saturdays than on any other day, and their fascination with the old-fashioned costumes always delighted me. I felt like I was imparting a bit of history to fire their imaginations.

But not today. Each time the doorbell rang, I checked the clock. The hours until noon dragged by. I shut the door behind my last customer at quarter of twelve and closed up for an early lunch.

Half a dozen people had already gathered in front of the Gulch. Someone—probably Frances, bless her heart—had put up barricades at either end of the street to block traffic.

Pastor and Enid Waldberg were there early. Dressed in period costume once again, with the addition of the prairie bonnet I had given her, Enid looked like the perfect prairie wife. She waved me over.

"Are you all set?" She spoke quietly. I'd told her the true purpose of the gathering the night before.

"I think so." I hedged my answer. "Put it this way. Keep your eyes open and your prayers sent heavenward until this is done."

"I always do." She smiled at me.

I spotted Dina and Suzanne by the swinging doors to the Gulch, not yet taken down since last weekend's festivities. Dina waved me over. "Hey, Cic!"

Suzanne leaned against the door. A wide smile shouting joy brightened her face. "I'll come get my dress this afternoon." She winked. "I heard about your date with Audie last night."

"Let me guess. You stopped by Gaynor Goodies this morning." As I had expected, Grace Gulch's rumor mill had done its work. Some date. We spent the night planning how to get a murderer to confess, but she didn't know that. Not yet.

Before I could answer, Audie called for our attention. Everyone had arrived.

"Thank you all for agreeing to come back today." His pleasant actor's voice carried without shouting. "We are going to try to reconstruct the events of last Saturday. We've asked you all to join us because you were in a position to see what happened. Mitch Gaynor and Mayor Grace have kindly agreed to take the parts that Cord Grace and poor Penn Hardy played. I will stand where Mitch stood on Saturday. Cici will take the mayor's place on the sidewalk."

I waved at the crowd and joined him on the right side of the saloon doors.

Everyone bustled around for a few minutes until they settled exactly where they had been standing when the gunfight took place. Cord turned around and shrugged. He had no assigned place, so he joined Suzanne and Dina by the doors. I spotted Frances across the street, her eyes tracking Mitch's tall figure as he headed toward the Gulch.

"Action!" When Audie shouted the word, I almost expected to see cameras on tripods rolling down the street. Of course they didn't. Mitch and the mayor disappeared behind the saloon doors.

Moments later, the two men burst through the doors, reading lines from the script Audie had provided. Without the benefit of practice, their voices didn't project well nor carry much emotion. Still, those of us on the sidewalk could hear well enough.

"You can't get away with it. You're a scoundrel and a cheat." As close as the words were to Mitch's threat, they didn't carry the same level of anger.

"I'm not a cheat. I arrived first, fair and square. And you have to accept it." The mayor, a political ham, couldn't keep the grin from his face.

They pointed guns at each other and pulled the triggers. Both men crumpled to the ground.

I held my breath. Tension twisted my shoulders, but I refused to turn around.

"Hand over your weapon, Mr. Howe—er, Gaynor." The chief of police addressed Audie, who had taken Mitch's place in the audience.

The audience whirled from the drama taking place in the middle of the street. The Colt in Audie's hand pointed straight at the spot where Mitch had been standing.

Surprised gasps erupted around me.

Mitch jumped to his feet. "Someone tried to shoot me?"

I took a step forward. "The same way you shot Penn Hardy during the gunfight last week."

Mitch pointed. "You're lying!"

I inched forward and landed within Mitch's long shadow. "You wanted to prevent Hardy from taking over the *Sequoian*."

"Stop moving!" Mitch waved his gun around.

I halted dead in my tracks.

"You'll never prove it."

"I think we will." Frances stepped out from the shadows. "As soon as we match the ballistics from that gun in your hand to the bullet that killed Hardy."

Mitch's face crumpled, erasing its normal civilized mask. He pointed his gun wildly. A puff of smoke exploded from the end of his weapon.

"No!" Audie yelled and jumped in front of me. We landed on the sidewalk, his long legs crushing my crinoline.

Around us people screamed. Audie did not speak or move. His chin dug into my shoulder. His stillness frightened me.

"Audie, are you all right?" I brushed my fingers across his back. I couldn't feel any blood. He still did not speak. "Audie!"

When Audie finally lifted his head, his eyes dazzled like sapphires. "I like holding you in my arms," he whispered into my ear, but it wouldn't have made a difference if he had shouted the words. Commotion made conversation impossible. He stood up and then helped me to my feet.

"If you cannot afford a lawyer, one will be provided for you at government expense." Frances Waller finished giving the Miranda warning to Mitch Gaynor. Handcuffs already secured his arms behind his back. The mayor shook Reiner's hand, congratulating him on bringing the case to a close. Dina lifted a camera to her eyes to capture the moment for the paper.

Audie and I did the work, not the police. But I could live with letting the police take the credit. The grapevine would spread the truth before an hour had passed.

I looked back at my sister. She waved at us and pointed to a small metal object on the wooden boards. One of the blanks from Mitch's gun, I supposed. Frances spotted it at the same time and retrieved it for evidence. Audie told me that he had triple-checked the guns for blanks and that they had never left his sight from the time he handed the guns over to the mayor and Mitch. We had tried to think of a way out of using the guns, but it felt necessary to pull off the deception. Mitch must have forgotten there were blanks in the weapon.

"Audie." I turned to look at the man who had placed his body in harm's way to protect me. "You could have been hurt."

"Blame Wilde again. 'Whenever a man does a thoroughly stupid thing, it is always from the noblest motives.' I forgot that the gun held blanks. All I saw was that the woman I love was in danger."

The woman I love. I looked at him, a silly smile spreading across my face, my insides melting from more than the midday sun.

Faces swam around us, and voices congratulated us on our part in the day's events. I heard their voices as if under water.

Only four words came through loud and clear.

"The woman I love."

September 30, 1891
Dear Mary,
Please God, this will be the last letter I pen to you before you become my wife. I am hard at work on our home in preparation for the arrival of my bride.

Ethan and Elizabeth Hardy promise to escort you to Chandler, where the preacher will marry us at his tent church. The trees are changing color; God Himself is painting the earth in preparation for our celebration.

God's grace has indeed reigned in Grace Gulch.
Your husband-to-be,
Robert Grace

Friday, October 4

"I lost my job." Dina sounded positively cheerful when she made her announcement at a celebration dinner a week later. Cord, Audie, and Suzanne joined the Wilde family for the evening. Even Jenna had returned for the event. "Without Mitch, the *Sequoian* is shutting down."

A moment of silence descended on the table. Regret

at the loss of a century-old community newspaper and the horror of local-leader-turned-murderer still appalled us.

"So Penn succeeded, even in death," I said. Frances had confirmed that the victim had been seeking to put the *Sequoian* out of business. "I guess Mitch decided to put an end to his takeover attempt. He figured that without Penn, his problems would go away."

"Were any of Penn's tactics. . .well, illegal?" Jenna asked. "I didn't think he had it in him."

We avoided looking at Suzanne. We hadn't told Jenna that tidbit. Adultery might not qualify as a criminal matter, although I had heard that adultery was still on the state law books as a crime. Who would sponsor a bill giving the green light to adultery? But it was still against God's law.

"Aside from having an affair with me, do you mean?" Suzanne brought the matter up herself. She laughed. Her hair fell in soft waves, framing her radiant face.

Jenna set her fork and knife on her plate and stared at Suzanne. "Really? I didn't know." She busied herself with her barbecued chicken and didn't say anymore. She was more sensitive about such things than most; she had never even revealed the name of Dina's father.

"And aside from threatening to publish that mad cow rumor?" Cord said. "It's libel to publish a lie, so technically it's illegal."

"Praise Jesus that's all in the past." The words fell naturally from Suzanne's lips. "It took losing Penn for me to realize that I needed the Lord in my life. I talked with Pastor Waldberg this morning and asked Jesus to be my Savior." Joy beamed from her face.

"Hallelujah!" Dad said.

"Praise the Lord." I touched her briefly on the shoulder, the hard feelings of a few weeks ago a distant memory as I greeted her for the first time as my sister in Christ.

A shadow passed across her face. "I only wish Penn could have known Jesus, too. I really did care for him."

"Maybe he did," Cord said. "He was a deacon at Word of Truth, wasn't he? Of course church membership does not equal salvation, but maybe he was saved and had just, well, drifted away."

Pastor Waldberg had officiated at Penn's funeral last Sunday afternoon. When I spied Gwen weeping in the front row, I felt guilty for having ever suspected her.

"To answer your question, Jenna," Suzanne said, "I don't think Penn did anything illegal. He liked knowing things about people. It made him feel powerful, you know? But he was very careful not to cross that line. He lived for the paper, and he didn't want to jeopardize that."

"Who's going to take over the *Herald*, I wonder," Audie said.

I knew the answer, but I waited for Dina to speak up.

"His city editor. A distant Grace cousin. She's offered me a job, by the way." Dina grinned. "So I'm not joining the ranks of the unemployed any time soon." Her now neon-orange hair could have lit the dark night.

Congratulations rippled around the table. "What will you be doing?" Jenna asked.

"I get to be a real reporter! I'll be following the Grace Gulch Bulls. Best of all, I get in for free."

I joined in the laughter. Dina loved high school football.

"Not only that, I get to edit the Grace letters. Oh, the editor will be looking over my shoulder, but she said I should have the chance since my family uncovered the truth." She tilted her head in my direction. "Thanks, sis!"

I hadn't heard this part. "Well done!"

"Has anyone objected to your publishing them?" Audie asked, looking at Cord.

Cord shook his head. "Old Bob left them at the newspaper for safekeeping, I guess. Only after his death, no one knew about them. Ron and Magda figure that he wanted the *Herald* to have the story. After they're published, we'll give them to the historical society."

"If you're all finished with congratulating each other, how about some dessert?" Dad pushed back from the table.

We followed him into the kitchen. Everybody had brought a different variety of pecan pie—part of the official state of Oklahoma menu. I brewed a fresh pot of coffee, glad I had stayed with twenty-first-century casual wear for the day. For once, I could enjoy the bountiful spread without worrying about my corset.

Suzanne ate the least and said an early good-bye. "Thank you so much for including me tonight." She hugged me. She hugged Audie and Cord, and then Dina and Jenna. She would have grabbed Dad if he hadn't taken a step back. "I guess we're family now."

"Amen, sister!" Audie smiled fondly at her. "I'm so glad you know the Lord now." He held up her coat for her to slip it on. I was pleased that no hint of jealousy marred my happiness.

She hugged me again on the way out and whispered in my ear, "Hold on to that one, girl. He's a keeper."

We decided to play Trivial Pursuit, the Silver Screen edition. Dina followed me to my old bedroom where we kept the board games and hugged me. "Thanks for everything, sis."

"I didn't do much."

"You just made sure no one blamed me for Penn's death, and you found the real killer. That's something." She blinked her eyes. "You came through for me, just like you always have."

I sat on my bed, which was covered with a crazy quilt, one of the last things Mom made before she died. I had tried so hard for so long to make up for the lack of a mother in Dina's life. "Someone had to."

Dina joined me on the bed and ran her hands over the quilt. "I know it was tough for you when Mom died. And I know you think I always preferred Jenna."

"That's only natural."

"Well, yeah, Jenna gave birth to me, and she's a lot of fun, but you—you've always been there, rain or shine. I'm sorry it took a murder investigation for me to see it." She hugged me again then jumped off the bed. "We'd better get back out to the living room before they send a search party."

Even with a full complement of players, I still won

the game. I usually did.

"You have an unfair advantage," Dina grumbled. "You associate all those movie stars with their costumes."

"You're just jealous because I won." I tugged lightly on her wild orange hair.

"I'd better get going," Cord said. "Dawn comes early for us ranchers."

I walked with him to the door. "I'm glad you could come tonight, Cord."

"Are you sure?" He managed a crooked smile.

"We couldn't have solved the crime without you. You helped us to figure out the angle of the gunshot."

"That's not what I meant." He nodded toward the kitchen, where Audie stood rinsing plates and talking to Jenna. "I felt like a fifth wheel."

It was time to clear the air. I leaned forward and whispered something in his ear before kissing him on his cheek. I waited on the porch until his truck turned at the end of the driveway. With him went a chunk of my history.

Audie came up behind me on the porch. A breeze pushed cold air beneath my cotton shirt, and I shivered. He slipped his arms around me.

"You and Cord seemed deep in conversation." Audie sounded uncertain.

I snuggled closer in his arms. "Oh, I just told him that he would always be my friend, but. . .that was all we'll ever be."

I felt vibrations in his arms. He spun me around, his eyes boring into mine. Unable to move, I looked at him, hoping my expression said what my lips did not. A smile I'd grown to love spread across his face, opening into a wide grin.

"That's all right, then." He pulled me closer and kissed me. For an eternity, I felt the promise of the first redbuds of spring, the warmth of a summer rain, the fulfillment of the peach harvest in fall.

"There's one thing—besides his lifestyle—where I disagree with Wilde," Audie said after a very long time.

"Really? What's that?"

"He said that 'a man can be happy with any woman as long as he does not love her.' He got that one totally wrong." Audie cupped my chin with one hand. "I happen to share King Lemuel's opinion. 'A wife of noble character who can find? She is worth far more than rubies.' "

He locked his cobalt gaze on mine, his eyes as intense as the fire of any precious gem. "I believe that I've found that special woman, and I intend to spend every day of the rest of my life making her shine."

I couldn't wait.

Award-winning author and speaker **Darlene Franklin** resides in the Colorado foothills with her mother and her Si-Ti (Siamese/Tiger) cat, Talia. Her daughter lives nearby, and her son and his family make their home in Oklahoma. She loves music, reading, and writing. Barbour published her first book, *Romanian Rhapsody*, in 2005. She also writes magazine articles, devotionals, and children's curriculum. Check out her Web site at www.darlenehfranklin.com.

You may correspond with this author by writing:
Darlene Franklin
Author Relations
PO Box 721
Uhrichsville, OH 44683

A Letter to Our Readers

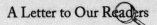

Dear Reader:

In order to help us satisfy your quest for more great mystery stories, we would appreciate it if you would take a few minutes to respond to the following questions. We welcome your comments and read each form and letter we receive. When completed, please return to:

Fiction Editor
Heartsong Presents—MYSTERIES!
PO Box 721
Uhrichsville, Ohio 44683

Did you enjoy reading *Gunfight at Grace Gulch* by Darlene Franklin?

Very much! I would like to see more books like this! The one thing I particularly enjoyed about this story was:

_____
_____
_____

Moderately. I would have enjoyed it more if:

_____
_____
_____

Are you a member of the HP—MYSTERIES! Book Club?
◯ Yes ◯ No

If no, where did you purchase this book?

_____

Please rate the following elements using a scale of 1 (poor) to 10 (superior):

___ Main character/sleuth   ___ Romance elements

___ Inspirational theme   ___ Secondary characters

___ Setting   ___ Mystery plot

How would you rate the cover design on a scale of 1 (poor) to 5 (superior)? _____

What themes/settings would you like to see in future **Heartsong Presents—MYSTERIES!** selections? _____

_____

_____

_____

Please check your age range:
- ○ Under 18   ○ 18–24
- ○ 25–34   ○ 35–45
- ○ 46–55   ○ Over 55

Name: _____

Occupation: _____

Address: _____

E-mail address: _____